FROM THE LIBRARY OF

Kayla
Eden

A NOVEL

Ella

A NOVEL

JESSILYN STEWART
PEASLEE

Sweetwater Books
An Imprint of Cedar Fort, Inc.
Springville, Utah

ISBN 13: 978-1-4621-1745-1

Published by Sweetwater Books, an imprint of Cedar Fort, Inc.
2373 W. 700 S., Springville, UT 84663
Distributed by Cedar Fort, Inc., www.cedarfort.com

LIBRARY OF CONGRESS CATALOGING-IN-PUBLICATION DATA

Peaslee, Jessilyn Stewart, 1979- author.
Ella / by Jessilyn Stewart Peaslee.
    pages cm
Summary: Dreaming of a better life than being treated like a servant in her own home, Ella Blakeley feels a glimmer of hope when she hears that charming Prince Kenton has announced a grand ball.
ISBN 978-1-4621-1745-1 (perfect bound)
[1. Fairy tales.] I. Title.
PZ8.P3El 2015
[Fic]--dc23
                              2015023701

Cover design by Rebecca J. Greenwood
Cover design © 2015 by Lyle Mortimer
Edited and typeset by Melissa J. Caldwell and Sarah Barlow

Printed in the United States of America

10 9 8 7 6 5 4 3 2 1

Printed on acid-free paper

For the *finders* of others' shoes.

We would be lost without *you*.

"If there is a real woman—even the trace of one—
still there inside . . . it can be brought to life again.
If there's one wee spark under all those ashes,
we'll blow it till the whole pile is red and clear."

—C. S. Lewis

Prologue

THE SOFT SUNLIGHT STREAMED IN THROUGH THE TALL eastern windows of Ashfield, illuminating the corn silk curls that bounced impatiently on Ella's shoulders.

"Can you show me now, Papa?" she pleaded, her tiny hands clasped under her chin.

Henry Blakeley smiled over his violin at his daughter and slowly pulled the bow across the strings, letting the last note linger in the quiet of the morning. The sound didn't pierce the stillness—it melted into it, transforming it into a more exquisite version of itself. He lowered his violin and bow, and his gaze turned from the brilliant sunrise and fell dotingly on Ella. He chuckled at her excitement as he set his violin on its stand and lifted her up into his arms.

"Up you go, Pumpkin," he said with a smile. He grunted teasingly. "You are getting so heavy! How old are you now? Twenty? Twenty-one?"

"Papa, I'm four!" she replied as she held up five fingers. Henry laughed and tucked her thumb down and Ella giggled. He carried Ella from the drawing room and into the foyer where they passed Grace, her governess, and Mr. Claybrook, the butler. Miss Bell was humming as she dusted the mantle on the opposite wall. Ella waved an enthusiastic good morning at them and they waved back affectionately. She heard the boisterous laughter of the cooks in the kitchen as they prepared her birthday breakfast and the luscious aroma of roasting ham and simmering maple syrup filled the house. Her tummy grumbled, but she could wait to eat. Henry had promised that he would show Ella her birthday present before breakfast.

Henry carried Ella up the stairs and she reached out her hand to slide it along the smooth banister. It always felt more like porcelain than wood to her. Henry reached the top of the stairs, continued down the hall to Ella's bedroom, and stood outside the door. Ella wiggled her dangling bare feet in anticipation.

"Close your eyes, Ella," Henry whispered.

Ella quickly covered her eyes and tightly closed her fingers, but then peeked through a crack in between them.

Henry reached down with his free hand and pushed on the latch, letting the heavy door fall open. In the far corner of the room, something glimmering caught Ella's eye. She couldn't pretend not to look anymore, and her hands flew away from her face as she gasped at the beautiful dress hanging on the outside of her wardrobe.

The gown was light blue: the color of the sky when it was covered with the thinnest layer of clouds—clouds that lightened the sky somehow instead of darkening it. Henry entered the room, walked past Ella's four-poster bed, and carried her to the dress until it was close enough to touch. Ella looked at her father, and he smiled and nodded his permission. She slowly stretched out her fingers and stroked the shimmering fabric. It felt as smooth as water when it flowed gently out of the well spout.

Henry watched his little girl admire the gown, a pleased

smile on his face. He kissed her rosy cheek and placed her on the chair at the foot of the bed. He walked over to the dress, took it off its hanger, and held it up to her, positioning the shoulders of the dress in front of her own. Even with her standing on the chair, the hem of the dress brushed against the floor.

"It's too big," Ella pouted, her lower lip poking out and trembling slightly.

"Of course it's too big, silly." Henry chuckled softly. "This is a very special dress and you must wait to wear it until you are a grown-up lady."

"I'll never be big enough," Ella said as she looked down at the yards of fabric swirling around her.

Henry grinned and reached up to touch one of her glossy curls. "Yes, you will." It was barely a whisper.

"Do you promise?"

"I promise," Henry said quietly.

Ella's smile returned. Henry always kept his promises. With a touch of sadness in his eyes, Henry turned away from Ella to place the gown back on its hanger. Ella sat down on the chair and was about to ask her father why he looked sad, but before she could, the expression was erased from his face and replaced with excitement.

"I have one more surprise for you, Pumpkin," Henry announced, his eyes brightening.

Ella covered her eyes and closed her fingers—all of them this time.

She heard Henry's muffled footsteps move across the rug and then his voice was very close to her. "Open your eyes, Ella."

She pulled her hands away from her eyes and saw her father standing in front of her, a smooth wooden box in his hands. The box was painted the same sky blue as the beautiful gown, and it had a white ribbon tied around it, holding the lid on tightly.

There were two letters carved on top of the lid: EB

Henry placed the box in Ella's lap and she lightly ran her fingers over the top and along the satiny smoothness of the ribbon.

"It's so pretty."

Henry chuckled. "I'm glad you like it. But I think you'll love what's inside."

She blushed and lifted the lid. Her lips opened into an astonished O, but no sound came out.

Inside the box, nestled in soft, white fabric, lay the most exquisite pair of slippers Ella had ever seen. Ella's fingers hovered over the beautiful shoes in the box, afraid that if she touched them they might burst like a bubble, vanishing into a million pieces. They were clear as a teardrop, but when they caught the light they glistened faintly with all the colors of the rainbow.

"Are they made out of fairy wings?" Ella whispered.

"Glass," Henry answered, pleased with her reaction. He carefully set the box down on the bed and lifted a slipper out. He knelt down in front of her and slipped it onto her tiny foot.

There were still a couple of inches for her foot to grow into, and Ella giggled. She sat admiring the too-big slipper on her foot and then gazed at the beautiful gown. "Did angels make these for me?"

Henry's gray eyes met hers and he whispered, "They once belonged to an angel." He paused, swallowing hard. "These were your mother's." He tried to smile, but his chin trembled and his eyes filled with tears.

Ella's heart quickly filled with the emptiness of missing someone she never knew. She looked back at the dress hanging in the corner. The sun shone on it and made it sparkle like newly fallen snow on a bright winter afternoon. She looked at the shoes that were as smooth and fragile as the pond when it froze over. She suddenly felt very close to her mother, knowing that these beautiful things once belonged to her.

Ella's gaze fell to the lid of the box next to her on the bed. "Does 'EB' stand for Ella Blakeley?"

"Close. It stands for Eleanor Blakeley." Henry said the name with reverence, his eyes still wet with tears. Ella recognized her mother's name and smiled. "I'm grateful that I can still hear her name every time I say yours."

Ella lifted her small hand and gently brushed a tear off his cheek; her face puckered in concern. He smiled and placed his big hand over her small one and held it there.

"You have her eyes, you know," Henry said. Ella felt his cheek lift under her hand as he smiled.

"They were blue?" Ella asked, her voice rising on the last word. She pulled her hand from her father's cheek and clasped her hands together under her chin.

"Yes. The color of forget-me-nots. But the most beautiful thing about your mother's eyes—and your eyes—is that they were kind. They were so filled with love and joy and compassion." He smiled, his own eyes far away. "I see her in your eyes every day."

Ella blinked in confusion as she listened to her father, wondering how someone could see kindness and love and joy in someone's eyes.

"Was she pretty?"

Henry's eyes were still unfocused, seeing things that Ella couldn't see. "Yes," he answered softly, staring out the window.

"Very pretty?" Ella's eyes twinkled.

Her sweet inquisitiveness brought Henry back to the present, and he turned to look into Ella's bright, eager eyes. "Yes, you funny girl. She was very pretty." Henry pulled on one of Ella's ringlets and it bounced back into place. "But your mother used to have a saying: 'Pretty is pretty for a little while, but true beauty is beautiful forever.'"

Ella pursed her lips. "How do you know if you're pretty or if you're beautiful?"

"I'll give you a hint." He reached out to playfully touch the tip of her nose. "You can't see beauty in a mirror."

Before Ella had the chance to ask what he could possibly mean, Henry scooped her up in his arms. "I'm going to have Miss Bell put your dress and shoes in a safe place for you. Then, when you're all grown up, you'll be ready to wear them."

Ella nodded soberly, trying to grasp the significance of her gifts, but she couldn't hold back a sigh of disappointment as she reconciled herself with the reality that she would have to wait so long to wear them. Her brow furrowed and she looked back at her father. Henry smiled at her solemn expression and Ella couldn't help slowly smiling back, and then bursting out in giggles. Suddenly Ella threw her arms around her father's neck and squeezed with all her strength.

"Thank you, Papa."

"I love you," they said in unison.

Ella laughed and pulled back to look at her father. "We said that at the same time!"

"Then it must be true," Henry whispered.

Among the Cinders

Chapter 1

ONCE UPON A TIME, I LIVED. NOW, I SURVIVED.

I sat on the damp bank of the small, glassy pond, unconcerned about the dirt and moss that were ruining my already ragged dress. I dipped my bare feet in the cool water and wiggled my toes around in the smooth, slimy mud. The tadpoles swam quickly away and hid in the cattails and under the lily pads.

Bright blue dragonflies hovered just above the algae-covered water: the humming of their wings both menacing and comforting. I tipped my head back so that my tear-soaked face could absorb the warm rays of the slowly rising sun. It seemed hesitant to rise this morning, unwilling to wake the world just yet. I understood how it felt.

I raised my arms and pulled my hair off the sodden ground so that it covered me like a blanket. Leaning back on my hands, I let my fingers caress the slipperiness of the mud and the soft, tender blades of grass that were trying to emerge but could never quite grow—their roots having nothing to cling to in the too-moist soil.

There was so much work to be done, but I couldn't pull myself away from this quite yet—the one quiet moment of my day.

Ella

Today would be a difficult one for everyone who lived at Ashfield, though not for the same reasons. It was the first day of September and ten years ago today my father, Henry Blakeley, had died. At that thought, I choked back a sob and turned it into a sigh, but not before yet another tear escaped and slid down my cheek. The pain of missing the most significant person in my world always seemed to hover around me like a fog, except for rare days like these when the fog became icy and sharp, piercing me from the inside. And though I usually would have fought against the pain, today I welcomed it. It helped to remind me that I was alive.

Victoria would be sad today too, or perhaps upset would be the better word; though not because she missed my father so much that it felt like the air had been knocked out of her lungs. Victoria was upset because with the loss of Father meant that he would no longer be adding to the considerable wealth he had accumulated while he was alive.

I wondered if Victoria would ever forgive my father for dying before he was able to give her all she had wanted. And—I shuddered—for leaving her to care for me all alone. Not that she had ever tried.

The sun was just rising over the distant hills, its bright rays finally deciding it was time to wake the slumbering countryside. The light and warmth helped me to pull my mind out of its melancholy reverie and open my aching eyes.

I blinked against the sun and the moisture that had been trapped behind my closed eyes, and allowed the tears to spill and clear my vision. I looked across the pond and saw the familiar and comforting sight of William Hawkins in his usual fishing spot. He had been away for a couple of days and I was grateful to see him there, especially on this day.

I absently wiped the tears from my face, raised my hand in greeting, and answered his smile with my own. His smile was so wide and so genuine it lit up his whole face. I marveled at how so much happiness could be contained in one person.

"Any luck this morning?" I asked as quietly as I could. I didn't want to scare the fish away, but I knew he could hear me; there was no other sound.

Will was leaning against his favorite tree, one leg bent up and his fishing pole resting on his other leg, his hat pulled low over his eyes. He was also enjoying the only quiet moment of his day.

"Of course!" he answered as he held up a long line of fish, dangling on hooks. "But I wouldn't call this luck. This is expertise."

"Of course." I smiled as I used Will's same words and returned to looking at the tadpoles that had slowly, cautiously started swimming around my feet again.

Will and I had both lost our fathers when we were ten years old. Only a few months after his father had died, Will had come to work at Ashfield as a stable boy so that he could help earn money for his large family. My father had taken Will under his wing, and Will was instantly drawn to him. If Father was out in the stables, Will was close at his heels, learning all he could.

He was fourteen when Father died and only a few months later, Will had stopped working in my father's stables. Not because he didn't enjoy the work, or that he wasn't a hard worker, or that he didn't know more about horses than any other man in the stables; but because Victoria had sold most of our horses in exchange for what she saw were more important things—like dresses, extravagant furniture, and trips to exotic countries. She had also neglected paying the servants and one by one, they left us.

Fortunately, Will had been chosen to work in the king's stables soon after. His knowledge of and way with horses at such a young age had more than qualified him for the job.

He loved the horses, but he would rather work anywhere else in the world than at the palace, or prison, as he referred to it. But once his older brothers grew up and left to seek their fortunes, the duty fell on Will to provide for the family, and he shouldered it with maturity and without complaint.

Will stretched, gathered up his gear and the fish he had caught, and headed toward the rickety bridge that extended across the width of the small pond. I knew it was time I should be getting home, and I reluctantly pulled my feet out of the water, rinsed off the mud, and tied my frayed scarf around my head, stuffing as much of my hair in it as I could.

My hands were muddy and stained pink from picking wild strawberries earlier that morning. I dipped them in the water and splashed them around, washing off the mud and hoping to wash away the stain, but knowing that it was no use. I dried my hands on my apron and picked up two full baskets of berries.

Will crossed the pond to my side and I met him at the end of the bridge. He looked inside my heavy baskets and his eyes widened. "When did you get up this morning? This must have taken hours!" He spoke cheerfully but watched me intently, almost warily.

I nodded. Morning had come especially early that day. I had spent half the night desperately trying to sleep, but every time my eyes closed, I was awakened by nightmares, and I would go back to staring at the comforting embers of the waning fire. Once the heat had completely faded from the fireplace and the chill crept into the cold stones of the dark kitchen and to my bare toes, I finally threw my thin blanket off me in frustration, pushed myself up off the hearth, and went to go do something more sensible than chasing sleep. I brushed the cinders from my dress, milked the cow, took her out to pasture, fed the chickens, and gathered the eggs.

But before I went to pick berries, I knelt down at the edge

of the garden, kissed my fingers, and touched them to the headstones of both my parents. I knew that this new day would mean the anniversary of Father's death and I dreaded it. And what I dreaded even more was the thought that I would be the only one who acknowledged it . . . or even cared.

"Yes, it was an early morning." I opened my mouth to say something else, but my breath caught in my throat and I closed it again.

"Ten years," Will guessed quietly, uttering the words I couldn't. His careful expression softened into compassion.

I nodded again and then smiled a little, relieved that I was not completely alone in my grief. I sometimes forgot how much Will had loved Father, and his expression reminded me of that. I blinked back the next wave of tears that threatened to spill over, knowing that if I let one fall now, they wouldn't stop. There was something tender about being understood that inspired tears.

"I'm so sorry, Ella," Will said gently. He lifted his hand, probably trying to figure out a way to comfort me somehow. He looked so helpless and I felt a rush of pity for him. I smiled my bravest smile and held out a basket of berries.

"These are for you," I said, and I placed the basket's handle in his still outstretched hand.

There was another moment of sympathy in Will's eyes as he watched my attempt to lighten the mood, but he smiled indulgently. "Thank you, Ella," he said softly, the sadness barely contained beneath his smile. "You always pick the best ones."

"This is for you too," I said, lifting the cloth that covered the basket and revealing a small tin pitcher nestled in with the berries.

"Cream?" he asked, his eyes sparkling in excitement.

I nodded, smiling at his enthusiasm for such simple gifts.

"I'm going to eat like a king!" he exclaimed. "You spoil me, Ella. You didn't have to do all this … but I'm also very grateful you did." He chuckled.

"You're very welcome. It's refreshing and enjoyable doing something for someone who actually knows how to say thank you. I think I would fall over dead if I ever heard those words at my house."

"Let's hope they never say it." Will laughed and I joined in. Will had taught me years ago that it was easier to laugh than to cry. He made it look effortless. Somehow he had overcome his grief and had turned it into something positive and even motivating. I tried my hardest to follow his example, but even now, when I did laugh, it felt like a hollow memory of what real happiness used to feel like and no matter how hard I tried, I couldn't recapture it.

"How was your trip? Is your mother well?" I asked, purposely avoiding any subject that could induce tears from me or discomfort for him. Will lived alone in a little cottage that he had built, his mother having left our village of Maycott to go to live with one of Will's sisters in the sea-bordering village of Lytton five years before.

"They are doing very well. Margaret just had another baby, and my mother is healthy as a horse." Will smiled like he had just told a joke.

"What is it?" I asked, my grin widening.

"Well," he stalled, trying to build the anticipation. "I sold the foal while I was in Lytton. I got more than what I was asking for him." His eyes brightened and he raised a hand to run his fingers through his hair, unexpectedly nervous as he spoke. "The man I sold him to wants the next one, and possibly the next one after that. Of course, once I can afford to, I'll be able to keep them and breed them myself."

"Will, that's wonderful!" I raised my hand and clutched his arm. "You've always wanted to raise horses! Your dream is coming true." I glanced down at my hand on his arm and dropped it, blushing at my overexuberance.

Will grinned back at me, not seeming to mind. "Well, not quite." He chuckled. "But I hope I'm headed in the right direction." A satisfied smile spread across his face. Will had worked for years to finally be where he was today. It had been a slow and often frustrating process, and even though Will only had three horses, the king himself could not be more proud of his dozens of horses.

Will's expression dropped slightly as he looked toward the increasingly brightening sky. He would soon have to be at the stables, readying the royal horses for whatever they would be needed for that day. I followed his gaze, feeling the sun's rays touch my face. It felt like someone's warm fingers against my cool, slightly damp cheeks.

At the thought of my cheeks, I gasped as I realized they were probably covered in muddy streaks left by wiping away my tears with dirty fingers.

"Oh!" I cried and ran to dip the corner of my apron in the pond. I scrubbed my face until I was sure it was clean. I pulled the apron away from my face, and sure enough, it was covered with dirt from my cheeks. I never cared too much about my appearance, but I certainly didn't want to *look* like someone who never cared.

"What's wrong?" Will asked, slightly alarmed by my erratic behavior.

"I'm covered in dirt and you've just been standing there looking at me not saying anything!" My once dirt-covered cheeks were now blotched red in embarrassment.

"Oh, I'm sorry. I didn't notice." He seemed sincere, but I shook my head, a touch of disbelief in my expression. Either he had noticed my mud-streaked face and was just trying to be nice, or he truly hadn't noticed and it was just another example of how Will could look past the bad and see the good. Either way, I was grateful for his kindness. I bent to pick up my basket of berries. Will looked down at his own basket and pitcher of cream and back at me.

"You're a good friend," we said at the same time, and then we laughed out loud.

"Then it must be true," I said.

Will's smile softened and he nodded, recognizing one of my father's sayings. He opened his mouth to say something, but hesitated, seeming to change his mind before the words actually came out. "Are you going into town today?"

"I don't think so. I have so much to do at home." I thought of the soap I had to make before Sunday, the worn-out dresses I had to weave into yet another rug, the butter that had to be churned . . . but then I observed the too-innocent expression on his face. "Why? Is anything important happening?" I smirked at the unlikeliness of that.

"You know I don't pay any attention to what they talk about inside the palace. It's just a lot of tedious royal blather." Will was rarely reluctant in hiding his distaste for what he saw as royal haughtiness and snobbery, but I noticed that it was Will who had brought up the palace, and not I. Something must be happening, but I pretended not to have noticed and tucked his comment away to think about later.

Will looked down in thought; then his brow puckered. "Ella, where are your shoes?"

I followed his gaze down to my bare feet peeking out from under my frayed hem. I was about to make a joke about it but couldn't quite manage. I kept my eyes on my feet as I shifted my weight between them. "I have to save my shoes for when I really need them. They're almost worn through. Besides, I can feel every pebble and twig through the soles anyway, so why bother putting them on?"

I tried to laugh, but it turned into a labored sigh. My shabby shoes were just another reminder of how much had changed in my life since Father's death. It had been long enough since his death that the drastic changes had now become commonplace and usually weren't shocking anymore. But on days like these, when I missed Father so much it felt like I couldn't breathe, it was impossible to ignore the differences. They practically screamed in my face.

I tried to read the expression on Will's face, but he abruptly turned away from me. We stood for a moment in silence, and then as if one of us had spoken it aloud, we knew it was time to go and we turned away from the rising sun. I waved good-bye and Will touched the brim of his hat, and we walked away in opposite directions.

Suddenly a shrill voice pierced through the stillness. "Ella!"

My head snapped up, my eyes widened with terror, and my heart filled with dread. My eyes darted to Will, but he wasn't looking at me. He was glaring in the direction the voice had come; the voice that could carry over the yard and through the trees, and yet, most often, would whisper menacingly in my ear and fill my heart with the same amount of fear.

In Will's eyes, I saw the resentment I could never allow myself to feel, the resentment that he had been trying to hide a moment ago when I had told him about my shoes. I closed my eyes for a moment. The pain I had let myself feel for Father dissipated back into the dull fog, and any lightheartedness I had felt while talking to Will faded. All I allowed myself to feel now was resignation.

I turned away from Will and started walking quickly toward the house and breathed a sigh that only the birds could hear.

Chapter 2

I BROKE INTO A RUN AS SOON AS THE ENORMOUS, IVORY-colored stones of Ashfield appeared through the clearing in the dense trees. This wasn't the carefree scamper of my childhood as I returned home after playing in the woods and into the arms of my father. This was a terrified run, fear moving my feet to the rhythm of my frantic heart. Instinctively, people usually run from danger. I had to run toward it.

My grandfather six generations back, Franklin Blakeley, had had the house built for his wife, Teresa. Ashfield had been in my family for hundreds of years and I took great pride in that. Though, it hadn't always been called Ashfield. It had originally been named Rosewood, for its beautiful roses and its close proximity to the ancient forest surrounding it. But, about one hundred years ago, it had burned almost completely to the ground and had to be rebuilt.

It took years to reconstruct and once it was finished, it was more grand and more majestic than it had been before. My great-grandfather had been so pleased with how the house had overcome a potentially devastating situation to rise from the ashes and become even more beautiful than it had been, that he had changed the name to honor the role the fire and ashes had played in its refining process.

"Ella!" My name reverberated through the tranquility of the morning once more from one of the upstairs bedroom windows, and I knew the fury that awaited me. I would have normally entered the house through the old servants' entrance in the kitchen, where my stepmother never was and where I now felt more comfortable entering anyway, but I knew the detour would only delay me more, and Victoria did not like to be kept waiting.

I reached the front yard, raced past the vividly colored roses that stood in brilliant contrast to the pristine paleness of the house, and hurled myself up the six steps of the porch two at a time. I pushed open one of the two heavy oak front doors of Ashfield—the one place I loved more dearly than anywhere in the world, yet it was also the one place where I was treated with harshness and hatred one moment, and in the next, with apathy and coldness. I tried to catch my breath as I carefully and quietly closed the great door behind me with a resounding thud. I could see no one at first, but I felt eyes watching me. With my eyes fixed on the marble stones at my feet, I untied my shawl and carefully arranged it across my shoulders, my hair falling loose around me. I set my basket of berries down on the floor and tried in vain to smooth my rumpled dress. Reluctantly, I raised my eyes to where my stepmother stood poised at the top of the grand staircase.

Victoria had one hand placed firmly on her hip while the other hand gripped the banister that had once gleamed white. Now, the paint was faded and the wood was warped and cracked. But the woman standing at the top of the stairs was a pillar of stone—cold, hard, and unbreakable. The contrast was chilling.

I waited in silence. I knew better than to speak out of turn and I also knew that Victoria liked to build the suspense by keeping me in fearful anticipation. I stood with my head high, feet firmly planted on the floor, eyes clear and direct without even a hint of bitterness or antagonism, but my hands trembled.

Victoria's perfectly set hair quivered slightly in her anger and her lips were a tight line. These were the only clues that told me how upset she was. Victoria always prided herself in being a lady and ladies never showed their anger, she would tell her girls. Her daughters, Mabel and Cecelia, had not quite mastered Victoria's carefully guarded façade. Nor had they given it much practice.

"Welcome home, child. Did you have an enjoyable ramble through the woods?" Her voice had returned to its normal volume now that I was back inside the house. It was almost too quiet—intentionally quiet—so that I was forced to really focus on her words. She spoke slowly, yet with subtle sarcasm, masterfully reining in any fury she felt. Victoria was not one to scream and shout, but the malice in her voice was enough to send a chill down my spine. I clenched my teeth and resisted the urge to shudder.

I jumped slightly at the sound of the bolt being locked behind me, but I didn't turn around. Out of the corner of my eye, I saw Mabel walk past me, a sly smile across her lips. She went to rejoin Cecelia, who had also been standing at the bottom of the stairs, watching the whole scene with satisfaction, matching expressions of abhorrence mingled with arrogance on their porcelain faces. I felt a trickle of fear in the pit of my stomach. But almost immediately, the cold fear was replaced by burning hot anger—anger that I had forbidden myself to feel. Did they really think that locking the door would keep me from escaping if I wanted to?

I silently chastised myself for allowing a few tears earlier. That sadness had opened the gates for the anger I now felt, and that was unacceptable . . . and dangerous.

By this time, Victoria had descended the stairs and was standing directly in front of me. I worked hard to keep my face blank and emotionless—like a mask—knowing that if she saw any anger or bitterness or even fear, she would use it against me to humiliate or punish. I silently cursed the flame that was coloring my cheeks. It felt like a betrayal.

Up close, I could see the wrinkles and creases that lined Victoria's once lovely face. It still would have been a lovely face, wrinkles and all, if her ugly thoughts hadn't crept their way out of every line, permanently mangling their owner.

But there was something in Victoria's face lately that showed a different kind of strain than ugly, angry thoughts. Her skin looked slightly sallow, her eyes sunken, the bones on her hands more pronounced, her collar bone jutting out from underneath her blouse. She had always been a slender woman, but this gauntness hinted at something more than the effects of a disagreeable temperament.

"You have kept us waiting this morning," Victoria accused in a menacingly subdued tone. "We are hungry." The very idea had Victoria trembling even more with rage. "I, the lady of the house, had to go into that horrid kitchen and actually search for food."

She had been in the kitchen! She *never* went into the kitchen! I felt my stomach turn icy, and I tried as hard as I could to hide the fear in my eyes, but I knew she had seen it.

She observed my reaction closely, probably not expecting it to be so intense. It was rare for me to show any emotion in her presence; I was rarely caught off guard since her anger and dissatisfaction with me were usually so predictable. But now, I stood there, hoping desperately that she would interpret my reaction as guilt for making her wait and not for the fear it really was. Whatever she saw on my face didn't prevent her from continuing. "And once I got there, can you guess what I found?"

I knew it was a rhetorical question, and I remained silent. I didn't know what she had found, and I fervently prayed it wasn't what I thought.

"Nothing!" Victoria spat the word out with venom. "Where is all of our food? Are you hiding it? Saving it for yourself as we starve to death?" She took one step closer and lowered her voice so that her words were meant only for me. "You're keeping something from me, I can see it. Whatever it is, I will find out."

Despite her threatening words, relief washed over me. She hadn't found anything; she hadn't discovered my secret. I never dropped my eyes from Victoria's vicious glare. After my initial panic, I kept my face as impassive as if Victoria were talking about the unseasonably warm day or whether the price of yarn had gone up again. My objective was not apathy or aloofness or disrespect. It was self-preservation.

"Please forgive me, Stepmother. You usually aren't awake yet." I pursed my lips and winced slightly. As soon as the words were out of my mouth, I regretted them. I was only stating a fact, but in my stepmother's ears, I had just called her indolent.

Without looking away from me, Victoria reached into her pocket. When she pulled out her hand, her long fingers were clutching the notorious stick she kept there for such an occasion as this, and I held out my hands. It wouldn't be the first time I prepared a meal with freshly whipped palms, and I had stopped hoping long ago that it would be the last.

What Victoria didn't know, what she refused to see, was that the only reason we had any food to eat at all was because I got up before dawn every day and milked the cow (our one cow), gathered eggs from the chicken coop (which now housed only two chickens), and picked berries. Then I would return to the kitchen and try to make a decent breakfast.

I would scramble, fry, poach, or boil the meager harvest of eggs. I would separate the cream from the milk and churn it into butter to put on the biscuits that I would make with whatever flour I could scrape out of the bottom of the barrel. Victoria was right. There was no food in the kitchen, unless one knew how to make something out of what they found there and was willing to do the work to put it there in the first place.

Victoria had accused me of wanting them all to starve to death, but it was because of me that they were even alive at all.

Still studying me sharply, Victoria pointed a bony finger in the direction of the kitchen and I was all too happy to escape. I quickly gathered my berries, trying not to flinch as I grasped the handle, and hurried to the kitchen, Mabel and Cecelia's soft cackles echoing in the barren foyer. Once I entered the kitchen doorway and was safely hidden behind the stone walls, I glanced over my shoulder to make sure I hadn't been followed. I carefully surveyed the kitchen to see where Victoria might have been searching for food while I was gone. A few bowls had been moved and some pans were out of place, and it appeared she had thrown a spoon across the room, but other than that, everything was where it should be. My heart slowed and I was able to prepare breakfast as usual.

When their meal of eggs, berries, and biscuits was ready and set out on the formal dining room table, Victoria and her daughters sat down grandly to eat. I was always amazed, and not in an admiring sort of way, by how she could act like nothing was the matter when something obviously was the matter. She had just given me a sound whipping and accused me of trying to starve them to death. And now she sat before me like this was the first time we had seen each other all day. It made my head spin.

As was expected and ordered of me, I stood in my usual spot in the corner of the room, waiting for the other three to be finished, so that I could clear their plates and take them to the kitchen. As I waited, I observed the fading yellow wallpaper that was peeling away from the walls in all four corners of the room and at the edges of each strip. If anyone looked at the wallpaper now, they would never know that there had once been dainty white flowers painted into the pattern. I daydreamed about tearing down the wallpaper and imagined how it would feel in my fingers. Would it crumble to dust or would it be stiff like tree bark? I would have torn it down years ago, but I was afraid of making it worse.

"We're going to call on the Wallaces this morning, girls," Victoria said as she bit daintily into her biscuit, gingerly dabbing with her napkin at the crumbs that had fallen onto her lip. "Mabel, wear your green chiffon and, Cecelia, your blue. Wear a brooch over the missing top button—that still hasn't been mended."

As she said this, she glared at me for the tiniest instant. It was true I hadn't been able to replace that button yet, but I didn't have any left.

"The Wallaces' second son, Roger, has returned from his tour and I want you to look your part. Every maiden in the village is after him, and I will not have my girls lose him to some shopkeeper's daughter."

"We can't both marry him," Mabel said sardonically as she placed a berry on her tongue, her pinky finger pointing out as if she were holding a teacup.

Victoria's eyes bulged and her lips tightened into a thin line. She glowered at Mabel until she was forced to look her mother in the eye. And even then, Victoria didn't look away until Mabel's eyes fell back to her plate. Cecelia watched the whole exchange with satisfaction, seemingly proud of herself for having the sense not to be disrespectful to her mother. Even I was shocked that Mabel had been so bold. No one disrespected Victoria. I was slightly jealous that Mabel could get away with only a glare. I would have been locked in the cellar for days.

Once the three women were done eating, they pushed away from the table and left without saying a word, to me or to each other, as usual. I quickly cleared the table and then followed them up the stairs to help them fix their hair and get them dressed for their outing. As I pinned Cecelia's brooch on, she smirked at me, obviously remembering Victoria's not-so-subtle rebuke from breakfast. I pretended not to notice.

As I dressed Victoria, I noticed how easily the buttons fastened and that her shoulder blades stuck out slightly. It puzzled me, and I silently reminded myself to put extra butter on her biscuits the next morning. I also noticed that the seam was coming loose at her right shoulder. I wouldn't have time to sew it and I was afraid of pointing it out to her, so I suggested she wear a shawl, without telling her the reason why.

Once the three women were dressed, combed, and braided, they left. I stood at the top of the stairs, reveling in the stillness. My fellow occupants were very rarely loud; in fact, there was an almost constant uncomfortable silence in the house, but when they were gone, the quiet was replaced with an unspeakable peace. It was the only time I could really breathe.

As soon as the door closed, I started humming tunelessly. Victoria hated music and expressly forbade me to sing. There were few things that reminded me more of Father than music, and I suspected it was the same for Victoria. Father had loved music and if he ever had a free moment, or needed one, he played his violin. He never needed any sheet music to read. He would simply wander from room to room, playing whatever his mood or surroundings inspired. He had played at parties we had held when I was a little girl, and for Victoria when he had brought her home to live with us. I didn't know if Victoria hated music because she had never really loved my father and music irritated her because it forced her to remember him, or if she really had loved him and it brought her pain.

In the past, when Victoria and her daughters used to leave to go calling, or to town, I would immediately drop whatever I was doing to go play Father's violin. It was in those times that I felt closer to him than any other. He had told me shortly before his death that I had a gift from God and that I must develop and cherish it. Father had taught me how to play from the time I could hold the bow in my tiny fingers. He would chuckle when I couldn't reach all the strings and promised me that it would come in time.

Sometimes I would play happy tunes to accompany the hopping, chirping birds that fluttered around in the trees. Or I would play dark and somber songs as I watched storm clouds blanket the sky in gloom. Both were therapeutic and gratifying, even the more subdued melodies. In them I could let the melancholy escape through my fingers instead of letting it fester in my heart. The resonance of the violin sounded hauntingly like the cry of a human voice, even when I couldn't let myself cry.

But six years ago, our situation had become dire. Victoria and her daughters had accumulated considerable debt at the various shops in town and after their many extravagant tours of other kingdoms and countries. Victoria had begun selling anything in the house that had any value to pay her debts. But I would not allow her to sell the violin. I would have rather starved to death than to watch it be sold. She had repeatedly demanded that I give it to her, but I had told her I didn't know where it was. We both knew I was lying, but my resolve gave me courage. I had wrapped it in cloth and hidden it behind a barrel of potatoes in the cellar.

I was fourteen years old. I stood in the drawing room, polishing one of the few candelabras we had left, when Victoria had gone with Mabel and Cecelia to town. I listened for the door to close and then waited for a few minutes. Once I was sure that they had gone, I dashed to the cellar, threw open the doors, climbed down the ladder, and pulled my carefully wrapped violin out from behind the potatoes. I didn't know how long everyone would be gone, but I only needed time to play one song—Father's favorite.

I glanced up to the open doors of the cellar to make sure I was alone. I tightened the bow and tuned the violin strings. Father had said I had perfect pitch. I smiled as I remembered the confidence he always had in me. I placed the violin securely under my chin. It had always felt like it had been molded perfectly to fit me.

I glided the bow over the strings and felt the comforting reverberations against my fingers, down my arms, and through my body. As soon as I played the first notes, the tears flowed—and not because my hands stung with the pain of my most recent whipping, but because I could hear my father's voice with every note. I closed my eyes, having played the melody a hundred times. I felt my tears splash onto the violin but kept playing, grateful for this rare opportunity to remember my father with no interruptions or judgments.

I let the last note linger in the air, like a soft keening in the otherwise silent cellar. I slowly lowered my bow and let the quiet envelope me. I let the last tears fall and sighed as I felt the familiar peace pervade my soul and the weight lift off my shoulders.

I never felt alone when I played the violin, but at this

particular moment, I felt even less alone. Uneasily less alone. Dreadfully less alone. Like someone was standing right behind me. As soon as I thought it, I knew it was true. I closed my eyes and shivered as the fear turned my blood to ice. I willed my eyes to open and forced myself to turn and face the cold blue eyes I dreaded most staring at me.

The most frightening thing about those eyes was that they didn't look angry. They looked empty. It looked as if she had politely listened to my song and now that it was over, she simply had no opinion of it.

After staring at me for a moment, Victoria had turned away from me, climbed up the ladder, and locked the cellar doors behind her without a word, without even demanding that I give her the violin. But I knew that didn't mean it was over. Her silence was a sure sign that there would be a consequence and that it would be far worse than any whipping.

I listened until her footsteps faded to silence above me. A part of me knew it was useless, but I groped in the darkness and wrapped the violin back in its cloth and put it back behind the potatoes. She left me there for the rest of the day and through the night.

The next day when Victoria came down into the cellar, I stood motionless as she searched for the violin, praying she wouldn't find it. My heart stopped in my chest when I saw her reach behind the potatoes and retrieve the violin. With an agonized cry, I grabbed for it and for one wild moment I imagined smashing it to pieces before she could use it for something as vile as paying off her debts. She pried it out of my fingers and climbed up the cellar ladder. I ran after her, grabbing the ends of her skirts, screaming and crying. She kicked me back and locked the door behind her and I spent another day in the darkness.

Victoria went to town, sold the violin, paid off their debts, and even had some money left over to buy her girls new dresses. To me, it felt like blasphemy and it cut to my soul.

I was finally let out of the cellar so that I could make them dinner. When it was dark, and everyone else was in bed, I had escaped out the back door and had run to the wig shop in town. The wigmaker was just locking her doors when I stopped her.

"Please, ma'am. Will you please cut my hair? I need to earn some money to buy back my violin." I blurted out breathlessly.

"Cut *your* hair?" she had said. "You're too young to be worrying about such things as money, child. Now run along home." She seemed confused, understandably, that the daughter of the late Henry Blakeley had come begging for such a thing.

I pleaded with her again, knowing it was hopeless and that the more she knew about our desperate situation, the more Victoria would punish me. Once I had that realization, I immediately stopped my pitiful begging and resigned myself to the fact that my father's violin was gone. I had been forbidden to ever reveal that we had become almost destitute or to ever ask anyone for help, and Victoria would not tolerate my betrayal. If Victoria ever learned of this, the consequences would be severe.

The wigmaker saw my desperation and her confusion melted away into pity, and once I recognized the pity on her face, I hated it. It only emphasized my powerlessness. I returned home in despair and cried myself to sleep on the blackened hearth.

Once Victoria sold the violin, I got a deeper glimpse at the callousness of her nature and I knew that she had no respect for things that were dear to me. My violin had been one of three treasured possessions of mine. Once I had lost that one, I had hidden away the other two out of Victoria's clutches and even knowledge. She had never known about them before that time, and I was determined that she never would.

Without my violin to comfort me, I had started singing and it lightened my spirits like the violin had, though a bit less powerfully. Even if Victoria forbade me from singing, she didn't have to know I still did when she couldn't hear me.

Six years had passed since Victoria took my violin. Today when I looked around me and saw the empty coldness in my home where there had once been warmth and laughter, I could take a deep breath and hum quietly to myself and feel like I was inviting a trace of that happiness back in, even if it was just to my own heart. I hummed as I gathered the dirty laundry off the floors of the bedrooms, and I hummed as I bent over the washboard and scrubbed the dirty clothes and hung them to dry.

Returning to the kitchen, I got started on leaching the lye out of the ashes from the sugar maple branches I had burned so I could make soap, and was surprised and slightly dismayed that Victoria and her daughters were already home from calling on the Wallaces. They couldn't have been gone for more than an hour or two.

There seemed to be a change in the air, and I walked out into the foyer where I had a view of the upstairs bedrooms. Mabel and Cecelia were excitedly running back and forth to each other's rooms, chortling outrageously. *Perhaps Roger Wallace had shown an interest in one of them*, I thought hopefully.

"Ella." I flinched at the sound of my name and spun around to face Victoria. She acted cool and composed, but beneath her calm demeanor, there was a sense of urgency. I noticed she still had her gloves on from when they had just gone out, and she was straightening her shawl.

"We are going to town." That was all she said. This was her way of inviting me to come, without actually saying it. And I wasn't invited because she enjoyed my company so much; it was because they needed someone to carry their things back home. If she hadn't expected me to join them, they would have left without a word.

I rushed out to the garden to harvest whatever I could so I could trade the vegetables for things we needed. The dirt dug into my sore palms and made my eyes water. I quickly filled my basket with carrots, cabbages, and squash and hurried back into the house. I would have liked to change into something more suitable to wear to town instead of staying in my plain gray dress and dingy apron, but I had traded my last dress for the bucket of flour we had just finished.

I comforted myself with the thought that I still had a dress that was too beautiful to wear, too beautiful to touch, too beautiful to mention to anyone.

Chapter 3

THE WALK INTO TOWN WAS A LONG ONE. WHEN VICTORIA was getting rid of Father's horses after his death, she realized it would be wise to keep one of them to pull the carriage. Old Gus. Unfortunately, last winter I had been forced to sell Old Gus in exchange for Lucy, the milk cow we now had. Our other cow had died and we needed the milk. Lucy was now one of the main reasons we were not starving to death, so I didn't regret my decision to get the cow instead of keeping a horse just to pull us around. Horses were more expensive to feed anyway. That's what I kept telling myself. In reality, it had broken my heart to get rid of the last horse Father had raised, but I had to do what needed to be done.

I had been thoroughly punished for making that decision without Victoria's permission. I still had the scars on my back. But I had purposely done it secretly and had known there would be a drastic consequence. I knew it was the only way to save us and Victoria would never understand enough to see how necessary it was. Victoria did not, and did not *want* to, recognize how desperate our situation was. She especially did not want anyone else to know. To Victoria, the loss of Old Gus was a declaration to the world that we were poor, and she refused to accept any responsibility for making us that way.

Whenever we walked anywhere it was a blatant reminder to the other three of what I had done to them. On these occasions, Victoria glowered at me as if she would gladly relive my punishment, so I always trailed behind, avoiding her icy glare. Today, as I carried my full basket of vegetables on my bent arm, I noticed the holes in the basket and silently reminded myself to gather the cattail stalks at the pond so I could soak them and repair the holes.

Usually Victoria and her daughters walked in a line side by side, but today Victoria trailed behind her daughters, who walked ahead of her at a brisk pace, eager to spend money they didn't have. But there was something else driving the girls forward. Their giggling had increased in pitch and frequency, and it was beginning to give me a dull headache behind my eyes. They were usually more whiny and grumpy than giggly, and I wasn't sure which one I preferred at the moment.

I assumed we must be going to town because Roger Wallace was going to be there too. I never liked him much. I used to have to have dance lessons with him when we were children. After each lesson, while the adults were talking, he would throw mud at me and pull my braids. And as he grew, I didn't think he improved much. But his family was very rich, and to Victoria, that was all that mattered.

In the distance, I heard the sound of wagon wheels approaching us from behind. Without turning around to see who it was, I walked closer to the edge of the dirt road to give the wagon more room. The wheels slowed as they reached me and then they came to a stop. I looked up just in time to see Charlie, Will's horse. Charlie was fourteen years old and showed no signs of aging. His back was straight and his gait was smooth. His eyes were alert and friendly. Will took impeccable care of him.

Will had gotten Charlie from my father soon after Will came to work in our stables. Because Will had been such a hard worker and a quick learner, eager to do anything Father asked him to do, Father had rewarded Will's hard work with a horse of his own.

I had watched from inside the house from the large second-story window that overlooked the stables and the pastures. I couldn't hear what was being said between the two, but they stood close together, as they watched the gray, skinny-legged Charlie wobble around his pen next to his mother.

Father had reached out his hand to shake Will's hand, as if they had just made an agreement. Will stuck out his hand, shook Father's briefly, and then had thrown both of his arms around him. Father laughed and patted Will on the back and ruffled his hair.

I smiled at the sweet memory. Father was always so willing to give, so ready to reward anyone for a job well done, so eager to show people how much he believed in them and their potential. It was the perfect memory to help me recall all the good things Father had done in his life, instead of focusing on how much things had changed since his death.

"Whoa, Charlie Horse!" Will called. He chuckled at himself. Will had named his horse Charlie so he could laugh every time he said the horse's name. I laughed lightly with him. In so many ways, he was still like that ten-year-old boy in my memory.

I reached into my basket and grabbed a carrot. I placed it in my palm and held it out for Charlie. He breathed heavily out of his large nostrils as his lips flapped around and pulled the carrot into his mouth. It abruptly reminded me of how Cecelia ate her biscuits that morning and I pursed my lips tightly to keep from laughing. I patted Charlie on his smooth neck, thanking him for the little joke we just shared.

"May I offer you lovely ladies a ride?" Will knew that Victoria had no intention of accepting a ride from a lowly stable hand in a wagon, but he liked to mock her in any subtle way he could. I shook my head and grinned at his lighthearted audacity.

Victoria and her daughters turned and looked at Will with identical glares of loathing and distaste that were not lost on him. He only smiled even wider in return. He often found their haughtiness comical, especially when it was directed at him.

"Did you get off work early?" I asked, knowing that he would usually be working in the palace stables at this hour.

"Not exactly. I need to pick up some more oats for the horses." He turned to the other three women. "So, do you want a quick ride into town, or would you rather enjoy the anticipation while you walk?" He chuckled again.

Victoria stunned us all when she replied with a curt, "Yes."

Her *yes* was vague, but I knew her well enough to know that she wouldn't have answered at all if she had chosen to walk. She would have just disregarded him without a word and walked away. Mabel and Cecelia turned to look at their mother with their mouths hanging wide open while Victoria ignored them.

Will climbed down from the driver's seat and hurried to the back of the wagon. Victoria seemed to have a little debate with herself and then finally decided to meet Will who was standing there, smiling and waiting, his hand outstretched. Victoria's eyes were clearly looking anywhere but at Will as he helped her up. Will tried to hide his smirk when she wiped her hand on her dress when he let go. Cecelia and Mabel were still astonished by Victoria's acceptance of a ride and simply gaped at their mother the whole time, even while Will took their hands to help them up into the wagon bed.

I tried not to stare at Victoria as I attempted to figure out her acceptance of Will's help. It was completely out of character. I had never seen Victoria accept any help from anyone. Yes, she ordered me to fix her food and brush her hair and make her bed . . . but that was not because Victoria was weak. It was because she was to be obeyed. It was to show me that she had power and status and control. To Victoria, accepting help was a sign of weakness, and weakness was abhorrent to her.

It was almost an absurdity to think that Victoria was finally becoming humble in our desperate circumstances, as was the idea that she could admit to needing help, even in this small way. All I could figure was that she must be suffering more physically than I had supposed that morning, or that she was in more of a hurry than I'd thought she was to get to town. Whatever the reason, I was grateful that she had accepted Will's offer. And I suspected my stepsisters were too. Because, though they would never admit it, the soles of their shoes were dangerously close to becoming worn right through to the ground.

"So, you *are* going to town today, then?" he muttered to me under his breath when it was my turn to get into the wagon. I had no chance to answer. After all that had happened that morning, I had forgotten that he had asked me if I was planning on going. I thought it very strange that he and my stepfamily were suddenly so concerned about what was happening in town. Surely Will wasn't at all concerned that Roger Wallace was back in town, if he even knew.

Will offered me his hand to help me up into the wagon, and without thinking, I placed my hand in his. I winced visibly and inhaled sharply through my gritted teeth as my tender, freshly whipped hand touched his. His eyes shot down to my hand, and I jerked it away and hid it behind my back with the other one. Will closed his eyes and clenched his jaw, but he wouldn't allow himself to look in Victoria's direction. Instead, he stared down at the ground, trying to compose himself. I was grateful that Victoria was studiously ignoring Will and me, and Mabel and Cecelia were now staring at nothing, sighing in boredom as they waited.

After a few seconds of him staring at the ground and me silently pleading with him to not say anything about it, he raised his eyes to mine. His fury and outrage and pity had been replaced by a fierce determination that I couldn't quite understand. Then, so swiftly it left me breathless, and so gently it touched my heart, he placed his hands around my waist and lifted me up into the wagon. Without looking at me or anyone else, he returned to the driver's seat.

People rarely ever touched me. I was abruptly aware of this as soon as Will's hands touched my waist. I had never really thought about it before. I never went driving anywhere, so no man ever took my hand to help me into a carriage. I never danced with anyone or embraced affectionate relatives—who didn't even exist anyway. My parents were gone and so no one ever hugged or kissed me. I was surprised by this startling reminder of how unaccustomed I was to having someone close to me and, ironically, how lonely it suddenly made me feel. I sighed and told myself to stop thinking about it. He was just helping me into the wagon, after all. But why could I still feel the warmth from his hands?

As we drove along, Victoria seemed not to have noticed Will's and my exchange outside the wagon. She seemed utterly resolute to pretend she was anywhere else but sitting on a hay bale in the back of a rickety old wagon bed instead of in our beautiful carriage we once had. I turned away from her to hide my smile. I wondered how well she was succeeding in that as the little bits of hay flew into our eyes. I was just glad I didn't have to feel every tiny pebble that poked through my thin soles.

Victoria ordered Will to drop us off just outside of town. Actually, she whispered something to Mabel, who then called out the order to Will over her shoulder to drop us off outside of town. Will helped them out of the wagon, and Victoria and her daughters didn't even glance at Will, much less thank him. They walked away quickly before anyone could see them getting out of an old wagon filled with hay.

While Will was helping the other three out of the wagon, I considered quickly climbing up to the driver's seat and down the side of the wagon. I wanted to avoid any awkwardness about my hands, but I decided that would do the exact opposite. Besides, I'd probably rip my last dress in the process.

When it was my turn, instead of offering his hand as he had with the others, Will lifted both arms out for me. I smiled in appreciation and embarrassment as he gently lifted me out of the wagon and placed me steadily on the ground.

"Thank you for the ride, Will," I said before he could speak. I didn't want to talk about the uncomfortable topic of my hurt hands. And my sudden awareness of his closeness made me terribly nervous so I tried desperately to hide that by talking . . . too much. "That was very kind of you, and besides that, I needed a good laugh today." I described Victoria's face as she sat on a pile of hay in the back of the wagon. It was as if she had been sucking on a lemon and couldn't spit it out until we arrived in town.

"I would have given anything to see her face sitting back there." He grinned mischievously, and then his face become abruptly serious. "The way they treat you infuriates me." His eyes glanced quickly to my hands.

"I know, Will. But we both know that confronting them only makes things worse."

My mind went back to a few years before when I had inadvertently mentioned to Will that I had been locked in the cellar all day without food or water because Victoria thought that I had stolen one of her favorite necklaces. Will had stormed into the house and yelled at Victoria. All she did was politely listen with a conniving smile on her thin lips. When Will left, I had been thrown back into the cellar for another day.

Victoria knew how to punish those around her, especially me. She could have yelled back at Will or even hurt him somehow, but instead, she took it out on me, and he never forgave himself. That was the only reason he ever stayed silent when he noticed how I was treated—knowing that she would find a way to harm me more.

My thoughts returned to the present and I looked up to see Will nodding, obviously reliving the same memory. I could see my own powerlessness reflected in his eyes.

"There's nothing we can do. Life is difficult and that's just the way it is," I said. "But thank you for caring, Will. You're such a good friend to me." Will nodded again with a brooding look on his face and left to tend to his horse and wagon, as I walked into town alone.

Chapter 4

THE PLAZA IN THE MIDDLE OF TOWN WAS BUSTLING WITH merchants and customers when we arrived. Traders were trying to outshout each other in their attempts to sell their goods. Victoria and her daughters always reveled in the chaos and loved going from shop to shop. Here, they were in their element.

I had always been mystified by my father's attraction to my stepmother. From the very first time I met Victoria, I felt uneasy around her. She had come to live with us, but I felt like I was an intruder in *her* life. I always wondered how Father was so blind to Victoria's cruel nature. Even in the six months between their wedding and Father's death, it was plain to me that Victoria was not all what she seemed to be. She could silence me with one glare of her icy blue eyes, and in the next moment, she would be gazing at my father with all the affection of new love, at least her impression of it. I had wanted to tell Father about my fear of Victoria, but he seemed so happy, I hadn't wanted to trouble him. I just figured it would take some time for us to get to know each other better and then maybe I could see that Victoria was as wonderful as she seemed to be when Father was around. I waited for that day for a long time. It never came.

A part of me was disappointed in Father's blindness, until I saw Victoria in public. When Victoria came into town to trade and buy, she became the lively, charming woman that Father had fallen in love with. I could, of course, see through the façade, but to the untrained eye, her dichotomy was imperceptible.

Today as I traded my vegetables for a small sack of flour and a few buttons, I watched Victoria as she effortlessly drifted from one conversation to the next, making people laugh or gasp in response to whatever story she was telling— in which she was always the main character—and then she would leave at just the right moment when people wanted to hear more so that they would be anticipating the next time they would be graced by her presence.

I realized in these moments why it was so easy for Father to fall in love with Victoria. He couldn't stand the thought of anyone being insincere or false. So much so, he refused to believe that those qualities could exist in such a vivacious and lovely woman as Victoria had been . . . or pretended to be.

There was only one word to describe Victoria's public "performances."

Perfect.

Maybe it was because of Victoria's inexplicable behavior on the way into town, or because of the gauntness in her face that I had noticed that morning, but I couldn't help watching her closely as I was forced to follow her from shop to shop. Victoria seemed completely at ease as she wove in and out of the crowds, her daughters following closely behind as if they wouldn't know where to go if Victoria weren't leading them along. But as I observed her, I was concerned by the slight sheen of sweat on her brow and the stiffness of her motions, and how no one else seemed to notice.

After over an hour of following Victoria and her daughters, my arms full of their parcels and boxes, they finally stopped to visit with some more friends.

"Is it true? Is he really coming?" a girl standing near me asked as she hopped up and down on her toes and clapped her dainty hands. I didn't know who she was, but I was used to that by now. I had lived in Maycott my whole life, but since I didn't exactly belong to any social circle and the town had grown so much in the last few years, my stepmother and stepsisters now knew more people than I did.

"I've never seen him, but I've heard he's the most handsome man who ever lived!" another girl squealed.

"He's been away for so long! I've been dying to see him," another girl sighed.

"Who? Roger Wallace?" I asked. Everyone looked at me as if they didn't know I was even there until I spoke. Victoria rapidly looked around at each face of the women in the circle, mortification in every feature of her pale face. Then, abruptly, the women exploded into raucous laughter.

"Roger Wallace? Roger Wallace? Who cares about Roger Wallace?" Mabel said between fits of laughter. She wasn't even addressing me. She was looking at the faces of the rest of the ladies in the circle so that they too could join in her amusement at my apparent stupidity. My face turned bright red, and I awkwardly excused myself—though no one seemed to notice me slip away.

I was thoroughly confused now. Victoria, Mabel, and Cecelia had cared very much about Roger Wallace just a couple of hours earlier. The girls had worn their best dresses to his house so that they would be the ones to catch his eye. Then out of nowhere, Victoria and her daughters had hurried into town for what I thought was another chance to be near Roger. But I had been wrong, apparently. And it was not only us in town. It seemed everyone else who lived in Maycott, or ever had lived in Maycott, was here too.

I strode away from the circle of uproariously laughing women as quickly as I could and carried the packages and my sack of flour to the fountain in the center of the square. I sat down on the edge of the fountain, held the flour on my lap, set their things down at my feet, and pursed my lips in frustration. None of the things they bought were useful. We all needed new shoes and practical clothes and food to eat, but with each shop they bought something more frilly and ridiculous. They had run up more debt than I could keep track of, and I wondered how they would possibly pay it all back. I shuddered at the thought.

I pulled my eyes away from the revolting pile at my feet and looked for a friendly face. Across the square, I noticed Will loading up bags of oats onto his wagon. Close behind him were three girls, giggling and pointing at him. Will heaved a heavy sack onto his shoulder, and one of the girls sighed and placed her hand over her heart. Will must have heard because he stopped and looked in her direction.

She giggled again and batted her eyelashes alluringly. Will rolled his eyes and finished loading the sack onto the wagon. I laughed quietly to myself. Will was always unimpressed by giggly, silly girls.

Sometimes I wondered if I would be more giggly and silly if trying to survive hadn't made me more serious. I was generally content with, or at least tolerable of, my life, but over the past few years, I had grown more pensive and even solemn at times. It was impossible for me to know if that had come from maturity, or from the void left by losing my parents, or from the possibility that the surviving part of me was taking over the living part of me. It wasn't as if I never felt any real emotion; it just seemed like I felt everything through the fog that was my constant companion. I just did what had to be done, without being particularly sad or happy about it. Just surviving.

I was brought out of my reverie by someone bumping into me so hard they almost knocked me off my seat on the fountain, and then they obliviously went laughing on their way. I wanted to leave town as soon as possible to escape this dense crowd, but I also did not want to leave until I knew what was happening.

I was about to go and ask Will if he would tell me what piece of information I was missing when my eyes met the eyes of the wigmaker. She was sitting on a rocking chair just outside of her shop, the tip of one shoe pushing against the ground as she rocked gently back and forth. She was the only woman I had ever known who worked in town, and it was only because she had taken over when her husband died. In Maycott, if a woman ever needed to earn extra money for her family, she most often quietly took in some sewing, but the wigmaker unabashedly set up shop right in the middle of town. It was quite the scandal for years, but now, she was a prominent, yet silent and watchful, fixture in the community.

I could tell that she had already been watching me, and I waved a hesitant hand in her direction. Every time she saw me since I had begged her to cut my hair, she looked at me with that same pitiful look that made me feel like I was even more helpless than I thought I was. I knew she wasn't trying to be unkind—quite the opposite—but I had come to avoid her and her keen eyes. I would be forever grateful to her for never revealing our conversation to anyone, but I had never been able to find the words to thank her. I smiled politely and looked away, but I could still feel her pitying eyes on me. No one else in town looked at me that way. But they didn't know what my life had become, if they even knew who I was. She did.

As I looked away from the woman, I spotted Jane Emerson admiring some shoes through a shop window across from me. Her father had worked for my father when we were young and she had spent many days with me at Ashfield playing in the garden, reading fairy tales in the library, and picking wildflowers. I gathered up my things, stood up from my seat on the edge of the fountain, and walked over to her, carefully avoiding bumping into anyone in the bustling crowd. I only saw Jane on Sundays at church and when we both happened to be in town on the same day. I was especially grateful to see her today.

I crept up behind her, freed one of my hands, and tugged playfully at her long, chestnut braid that fell down her back. Jane's butter-yellow silk taffeta dress swirled around her as she spun around in surprise. When she saw me, her face broke into a delighted smile.

"Oh, Ella! You look radiant today! I think your eyes are getting bluer. How is that even possible?" She laughed and reached for a lock of my hair that hung loose around my face. I had taken it out of my scarf before we came to town, but didn't have time to braid it or put it up. "I love your hair in the summer. It's the color of corn silk." She stole a glance over my shoulder. "And I'm not the only one who sees how gorgeous you are."

I gave her a quizzical look, glimpsed over my shoulder, and spotted an impeccably dressed man leaning against a pillar. His hair was combed and slick, and a cigar was sticking out of his mouth. He was staring at me, his hands in his pockets and a leering expression on his face. Roger Wallace. He looked exactly how I remembered. I scowled and turned back to Jane, but she was still looking past me, captivated. I followed her gaze and to my horror saw that Roger Wallace had peeled himself off his pillar and was making his way toward us.

He threw his cigar on the ground, put his hand back in his pocket, and swaggered across the square. He didn't go around anyone. He walked in a straight line through the crowds and made them part for him, as if he saw himself as something biblical.

"Don't leave me!" I whispered to Jane.

"I won't," she said urgently, though we were both on the verge of laughter. But just then I heard someone call out "Jane!" and she was forced to join another conversation behind me.

By this time, Roger was standing directly in front of me. His eyes took me in from head to hem. I stood there helpless as he inspected me. He made no attempt to disguise what he was doing.

"Afternoon, Miss Blakeley," he said, touching the brim of his hat.

"Yes, it is."

His scrutinizing eyes narrowed slightly as he processed my less-than-ecstatic greeting, and he looked at me more closely, more menacingly. "You know, when I saw you across the square just now, I thought to myself, 'That Ella Blakeley is the most beautiful girl in the kingdom.' But now, up close, I see that the years have not been kind to you, my dear."

"I'm flattered, Mr. Wallace. I could tell from all the way across the square that the years have not been kind to you." I was shocked by my anger and that I allowed myself to feel it and even act upon it.

He leaned in closer and I was overcome with the stink of cigar smoke and brandy. He chuckled as he pulled out his cigar case and casually chose the perfect cigar, rolling it under his nose and inhaling deeply. He gestured to my packages, and his voice took on a cruel edge. "I hope you have a new dress in one of those boxes. You look like a peasant. A filthy, mad peasant."

He touched his hat once more and sauntered back to his pillar. I stared after him. I could understand the filthy part. But mad? That one stung. I could hear Jane saying good-bye to her friends, and I composed my face before I turned to her. I decided to forget that I had ever seen Roger Wallace or that what he had said bothered me. I went to help Jane look for shoes and my good humor returned.

"Why are you looking for new shoes? I thought your feet stopped growing years ago, like mine," I teased as we entered the last shoe shop.

"They did. But a girl can never have too many shoes!" Jane laughed, nodding her head at my packages that she, like Roger, must have assumed were filled with new things I had bought for myself.

I joined feebly in her laughter, suddenly aware of the large hole in the heel of my shoe and the way each pebble poked through my almost nonexistent soles. My laughter died away and was replaced by a content smile. I was suddenly reminded of—and comforted by—the memory of another pair of shoes. A pair of shoes I had owned since I was a little girl. But like my beautiful dress, no one knew about them.

As she shopped, I tried to ask Jane if she knew what was happening in town today, but she was thoroughly preoccupied by the task at hand. I helped her pick out the perfect pair of shoes, and she bought them with a few coins from her purse. As she closed her purse, she frowned at the one coin left inside of it.

"Oh, I would give anything to be rich," Jane sighed with longing. I smiled and shook my head affectionately. Jane's vanity was endearing. She didn't mean to hurt anyone; she was just completely unaware of circumstances outside her own untroubled life, and I understood that. She was sweet and innocent and had never really known discomfort or misfortune, and I was glad. I was grateful that she would never have to tarnish her sweetness and innocence.

Ella

The booming voice of Jane's father from behind us made us both jump.

"Jane, are you ready? It's almost time for the—Ella! What a wonderful surprise! I haven't seen you in ages. How are you, my dear? I was just thinking of you." I desperately wanted to ask him what it was almost time for, but then he went on and I was glad I didn't interrupt him. "It was ten years ago that we lost your dear father, wasn't it? Oh, he was a good friend, a very good friend, indeed! I don't think I've ever known a kinder, more wonderful man in all my life. Why, just the other day I was reminiscing with Mildred about the time he came over and brought us that delicious ham for Christmas. I don't think I've ever had a better ham in all my . . ."

I was absolutely delighted to hear that someone else had taken the time to remember Father. I was completely caught up in Mr. Emerson's jovial story when his voice was abruptly drowned out by the startling blare of trumpets. All conversation ceased. I gasped and turned away from Mr. Emerson and to the direction of the deafening trumpets. All I could see were gold and green flags fluttering high above the heads of the vast crowd.

The crowd parted and carriage after royal carriage rolled into the square. The crowd jostled around me to get a better view and I had to cling tightly to the packages in my arms. The carriages were a lustrous pearl color with gold trim and emerald-colored ribbons trailing behind them, and they were pulled by gleaming white horses. I wondered for a moment if it had been Will who had brushed the horses until they almost sparkled, and then I realized all these carriages must have something to do with whatever secret everyone knew about but me. I could feel my mouth hanging open in amazement at the scene in front of me and quickly shut it. But I couldn't do anything about the wideness of my eyes.

Abruptly the procession came to a stop. In the carriage directly across the square from me, a little man sat next to the driver. He had a pearl-white suit on with gold trim on the shoulders with an official-looking emerald hat on his head. If it weren't for his long gray mustache that curled up at the ends, he would have blended in perfectly with the carriages. He stood up, unrolled the scroll that was in his gloved hands, cleared his throat, and began speaking in a loud, nasal voice.

"Hear ye! Hear ye!" he cried.

I smiled, finding it amusing that he thought he needed to call everyone's attention to himself. Everyone was already gaping. "Announcing the arrival of Prince Kenton, who has traveled far and wide . . ."

As he spoke, a man climbed out of the carriage. He wore a long white cape that flowed over his impossibly puffy sleeves and his jaunty green hat was topped off with a white feather. He hopped down onto the ground, jogged to the fountain about ten feet from where Jane and I were standing, and leapt up to stand on the exact spot where I had been sitting a few moments before.

The mustached man had finished with his introduction, which I had barely heard any of because I had been fascinated by the man standing on the fountain, and now all was silent. He flashed a dazzling smile into the crowd and waved. A few onlookers waved back vaguely, but most just gawked.

"Let me introduce myself to you all. I am Prince Kenton. I have spent much of the last few years away from home, traveling the world, meeting fascinating people, and seeing magnificent things. I have been in the company of princes and kings, sultans and czars, emperors and rajahs. But," he paused dramatically, "I have come home." His voice was tinged with unexpected tenderness at those words and his eyes swept the crowd with a look of adoration. "And now I would like to spend some time with butchers, bakers, and candlestick makers," he said, chuckling.

I wasn't sure what he meant, but I glanced at the carriage the prince had emerged from and noticed that the curtains had been pulled back. I was surprised to see the queen and king sitting next to each other, exchanging a disapproving look. Whatever the prince was about to announce clearly had not been their idea.

"And so," he said, raising his arms out as if to embrace everyone in the crowd, "we are going to have a ball! And you are all invited!"

The crowd cheered. Some girls nearby jumped up and down as they embraced each other and squealed with delight. At the word *ball,* an image flashed into my mind of Father holding a beautiful gown up to my shoulders and slipping an exquisite glass slipper on my little foot. My heart raced and I couldn't catch my breath. I pushed the memory out of my mind quickly, almost as if someone would discover my secret if I thought about it too long.

I looked up to see the prince smiling in satisfaction at the reaction of the crowd. I sensed that there was more he wanted to say, but he was letting everyone celebrate the news for a moment. He raised his arms and the rambunctious noise instantly hushed to absolute silence.

"As you may know, I am almost twenty-five years old, and as is our custom—our law—I am to be married before my twenty-fifth birthday." I could have imagined it, but I thought I sensed a little resentment in his voice. "I have seen all I want to see of the world. I have met everyone I want to meet. I am ready to settle down—to marry the girl who shall one day be our queen."

The crowd cheered politely. We all knew that this time was coming soon, and some in the village had even wondered why it hadn't happened yet. It was a lovely announcement, and it was wonderful that he would be married soon and that we would know who our next queen would be. I was excited about the ball and his benevolence in inviting all of us, but I sensed there was something more significant he hadn't said yet.

The prince continued. "And it has also been our custom that royalty has always married royalty. But my dear father and mother and I," he said, gesturing to the king and queen seated in the carriage behind him, "have found that this custom is simply that—a custom. This is *not* a law." It sounded like he had stated that point a hundred times, perhaps even argued that point a hundred times. "So, in conclusion . . . I may marry anyone I wish." He paused. "And it may be one of you."

The roar of the crowd was deafening, but I hardly noticed. I didn't move or even blink when he made the announcement, but I was vaguely aware that girls all around me were screaming, some were crying, and one had even fainted a few feet away from me. I had not taken my eyes off the prince. For when he had said the word *you*, he had said it while looking directly at me.

For a moment I thought back to the conversation I'd had with Will when we had discussed my whipped hands and how I had told him that there was nothing we could do to change how difficult things were. At the moment the prince made the announcement, I felt a small glimmer of hope, like there might be something I *could* do to change things.

The prince was smiling again, seeming very satisfied with the crowd's enthusiastic reaction. His eyes swept around the cheering, crying, fainting crowd and his gaze came to rest on me again. I felt like I should look down, but my eyes wouldn't obey. I felt a blush creep onto my cheeks as his eyes locked on mine and held them there. He smiled a dashing smile, a dimple appearing on his cheek, and winked.

I simply blinked slowly in response, but it was enough to allow me to finally lower my eyes and attempt to hide my burning face.

From my lowered lashes, I could see the prince slowly look away, his handsome smile still in place. He raised his arms again and the crowd was silenced.

"The ball will be held one week from tonight," the prince continued, and I hesitantly looked back at him. He looked into the faces of his subjects and came to rest once more on my face. He stared in my direction until my blush reappeared, but this time I did not look away. "Let's all get to know each other a little better," he said with a grin, his voice low and attractive. I couldn't help the small smile that slowly touched the corners of my mouth.

The prince jumped down from the fountain's edge and walked back to his carriage as he waved at the crowd. This time, they waved back and even blew kisses without hesitation. Girls were pushing past each other to make sure they got one last look of him, or to make sure that he got one last look of them. With one last bow, he climbed into his carriage, the procession moved forward and they were gone.

Chapter 5

I STARED AFTER THE CARRIAGES AS THEY DISAPPEARED around the bend and into a choking cloud of dust. I didn't know where they were headed, but they could have been driving to the moon and it wouldn't have mattered. I was still reeling from the announcement of the ball, but mostly from the prince's winks and smiles directed at me. I blushed furiously and shook my head and scolded myself for my vanity.

Suddenly someone was pulling on my arm and jumping up and down. It took me a little too long to realize that it was Jane and that she was saying something to me.

"Did you see? Did you see?" Jane was squealing.

"I'm sorry, Jane. What did you say?" There was absolute chaos in every direction, but I felt like I was in a dream.

"The prince! The prince winked at me! Oh, I'm in love." Jane dropped her hands from my sleeve and began to spin around in slow circles, her eyes closed, her face tipped back toward the sun.

At first I was baffled that she would think he had winked at her. I was so sure it had been me who the prince had winked and smiled at. We had looked into each other's eyes.

But, as I looked back on it, the sun had been in my eyes and the crowd had been chaotic all around me; I suppose I could have been mistaken. I ducked my head in embarrassment. It had actually been Jane who the prince had noticed. The glimmer of hope I had felt began to diminish.

Why would the prince wink and smile at me, especially when I was standing next to Jane? She was elegant and well-dressed and refined and lovely. Even now, as she deliriously spun around in her yellow dress, she looked like a drop of sunshine in the middle of all the madness. I scrutinized my horrid dress and reached to touch my wild hair. I felt completely foolish and filthy.

I slowly turned away from Jane, who was now in a completely different world, and my face smacked right into Will's chest. I stumbled backward as I dropped my packages I had forgotten I was carrying. He grabbed my arms to steady me, but I was barely aware of his touch as a strange yet familiar numbness washed over me.

"Sorry, Will," I said vacantly. I looked down at the packages at my feet, knowing I should pick them up, but not being able to make myself.

He didn't say anything but made sure I was steady then dropped his hands. He bent over and started gathering up my dropped boxes despite my halfhearted protests. He stood up once everything was gathered, and before I could thank him, he began walking away in the opposite direction. He didn't say anything, but I assumed I was supposed to follow him.

As I finally started moving, my brain began to catch up with my body and I noticed how strangely Will was acting. "What's wrong?" I asked breathlessly, practically running to keep up.

He shook his head and dropped his eyes. "Nothing," Will replied.

He was a terrible liar. "Did you know about the ball?" I tried not to sound accusatory, but the question came out sharper than I'd intended. My injured ego was still healing.

"Ella, I work in the palace stables. I know things before the king does." He laughed without humor. Before I knew where we were going, we were at his wagon and he was loading the parcels into the back. I realized he wasn't going to let me walk home carrying all of that. I looked around for Victoria, knowing she would probably want a ride back home. I spotted her across the square, talking to Jane, who had stopped spinning. They were clasping each other's hands, and Mabel and Cecelia were giggling and smiling dreamily.

I had never seen any of my stepfamily talk to Jane before and I thought it odd that they would start now. I caught Victoria's eye and motioned to the wagon, indicating that our ride was leaving. She glared back at me with an appalled expression and shook her head curtly, then turned back to Jane who was now talking animatedly with Mabel.

I turned toward the wagon with a resigned shrug. If they wanted to walk, I wasn't going to force them not to. I was just grateful she didn't forbid me from getting a ride home. Will was waiting for me at the side of the wagon and I walked to stand next to him.

"No hay this time?" I teased.

He only shook his head and placed his hands on my waist—no doubt remembering my hurt hands—and lifted me gently up onto the seat. My cheeks burned again when he touched me and only added to the flame from my recent humiliation. Will climbed up next to me. Before he even sat down, he clicked his tongue and Charlie started trotting forward, the dust kicked up by the wagon creating an insubstantial barrier between us and the pandemonium.

We drove out of town in silence, but it was a pensive

silence permeated with our own thoughts, not just the absence of sound.

"Please tell me what's wrong," I said suddenly. "Why wouldn't you tell me about the ball? Everyone else seemed to know. Why couldn't I?" I knew I sounded like a whining child, but I was desperate for answers. Will never kept anything from me . . . well, that I knew of.

He sighed heavily. "Not everyone knew. They knew there was going to be an announcement from the prince; they just didn't know what it was going be."

It still didn't explain his strange behavior. "This is why you wanted to know if I'd be in town today?"

"Yes." He wouldn't look at me.

"You didn't want me to know about the ball?" I guessed, feeling confused and betrayed.

Slowly, Will shook his head.

I looked away from him toward the road in front of us. Anger boiled up inside of me, but almost instantly subsided. I knew this was so out of character for Will, but I also knew he would never deliberately be cruel to me. I pondered for a moment, trying to figure out why he would keep this from me and then smiled. "Will, did you keep it from me because you're worried I won't have anything to wear to the ball?" I asked, my tone becoming gentler.

His eyes met mine, but they were unreadable. He didn't say anything for a long moment. "Yes, that's it," he said simply.

"Oh, you don't have to worry about that. You are so nice to be concerned about me." I laughed, but tears filled my eyes.

Will nodded and his smile returned, though it was tinged with a reluctance so subtle I thought I imagined it. His eyes returned to the road. "I'm sorry I didn't tell you about the ball." He was quiet for a moment and then looked over at me with a sudden resolve on his face. "You should have the same opportunity as anyone else to marry the prince and I won't stand in your way of that. You deserve it, Ella. More than anyone."

I was touched by his sincerity and smiled at him gratefully. We reached the fork in the road where Will would drive back to the palace if he weren't taking me home, and I told him I could walk from here. He stopped the wagon, but before I could climb down, he hopped down and walked around the wagon to meet me on my side. He held up his hands for me as he had done before and helped me out of the wagon. But unlike before, he didn't immediately drop his hands from my waist when my feet touched the ground.

I looked up at him questioningly but dropped my eyes when I was aware of how close he was and that he seemed to have no intention of moving. I kept my eyes on the dirt road between our feet, biting my lower lip nervously, wondering what he was thinking. A moment later he dropped his hands.

"I can carry these for you," he said suddenly, gathering the packages from the back of the wagon.

"Don't be silly. I can almost see Ashfield from here," I said and took the packages from him.

He nodded, an unrecognizable expression on his face, and climbed back into the wagon.

"Thank you, Will!" I called as he drove away. He touched the brim of his hat and disappeared behind the bend.

On my short walk home, I daydreamed about the ball to distract myself from thinking about all the chores I had left undone. It wasn't difficult. It didn't matter if the prince had noticed Jane and not me. I was determined to go to the ball and have a wonderful time. I had never been to a ball or even had any reason to dress up since Father's death. When he was alive, there had been countless parties around the kingdom to attend, including many at our own home. I had worn adorable, ruffled dresses made with yards of material that hung just below the knees with starched petticoats underneath that made me look like a little bell. Grace, my governess, would spend hours getting each of my ringlets just right. But I wasn't completely ready until I was able to twirl and twirl and watch my skirts ripple around me.

I wondered how different it would be going to this royal ball compared with the parties of my childhood. I sighed longingly at the thought of wearing beautiful clothes and eating rich, delicious food. My mouth watered and my stomach grumbled. I frowned slightly, thinking of the food that awaited me at home. But the food was instantly forgotten as I tried to imagine myself in my most, and only, prized possessions—my gown and glass slippers.

Suddenly I was running. Not running with fear, but with giddy anticipation. If I got home as quickly as I could, I would be alone, alone long enough to try on my dress and slippers, to try to imagine myself at a royal ball. Then perhaps this dream would feel like a reality.

The sun was low in the sky when I saw the stately exterior of Ashfield in the distance, its towers glowing white like a beacon to me in the fading blush of sunlight. I bolted into the house, dropped the packages in the doorway, and ran through the foyer and dining room and into the kitchen.

I stood silently for a moment, making absolutely sure I was alone. Normally I never would have imagined that anyone would be in here, but knowing that Victoria had entered the kitchen that very morning made me extra cautious.

She had been right. I was hiding something from her, had been hiding something from her for ten years. From the first moment I met her, I could never imagine telling Victoria about these gifts that had once belonged to my mother. It started out as a reluctance to share something with this intimidating woman who had married my father, and it grew into a need to protect the things that connected me to my parents. I had been told that I had my mother's eyes, her hair, her feet, and her hands; I had my father's dimples, his laugh, and his love of music and horses. I was grateful for those things, but the dress and slippers were things I could touch and hold, and they helped to remind me that those people I loved were once real enough to touch and hold too.

I walked to the counter that stood in the middle of the kitchen where I prepared the meals and knelt down. Under the counter were cupboards where I kept the pots and pans. I opened one of the doors and pulled out three heavy cast iron pots and set them on the floor, revealing a small wooden crate that had been hidden underneath them. I paused once more to make sure I was alone, my fingers trembling. I gingerly lifted the crate out of the cupboard and set it on the floor in front of me. I pried open the lid and smiled.

Wrapped delicately in brown paper were the only material possessions I had left from my parents. It had been months since I dared to look at them. Lately, Victoria had never left the house long enough for me to risk it. It seemed especially providential that Victoria was out of the house today on the anniversary of Father's death. Today, I would get to spend time with him, in a way, and remember when he gave me my gown and glass slippers.

I pulled back the paper and let it fall, revealing the perfectly folded, incandescently shimmering dress that had once belonged to my mother. In the crate next to the dress lay the box that contained the precious glass slippers. I closed my eyes and tried to remember how clear they were, but also how they caught the sun and reflected a whole rainbow of colors. I lovingly untied the now-discolored satin ribbon and lifted the lid to reveal the glittering glass slippers. The falling sun shone in through the west window, casting a rosy hue on them both.

I had never tried on the gown or the shoes, knowing that I was too small for them until recently anyway, and not wanting to risk their discovery, regardless. But the knowledge that they were there for me whenever I might need them had always been reassuring to me. I had only occasionally touched them, but usually I simply looked at them and that was enough.

As my eyes shifted from my gown to my slippers and back, I was filled with the memory of when Father had given them to me. That memory was infused with light. Light from the gown that glistened as it caught the sunlight. Light that shattered off the translucent slippers and the rainbow they cast on the wall. Light from Father's eyes as he watched me accept my precious gift. And light and pure joy from the knowledge that these lovely things had once belonged to my mother, Eleanor.

My hand was poised, aching to hold the contents of my little hidden crate, but slowly, I let my hand drop onto my lap. Maybe I felt too dirty after such a long day and a walk on a dusty road. Maybe I was worried that the rest of my family would be home soon. Or maybe it was the feeling that brought tears to my eyes that spilled down my cheeks—that as I contemplated putting on the dress and slippers, I felt unworthy of such beautiful things.

I suddenly realized I no longer felt like the joyful little girl in my memory. That child was young and fresh and clean. She hadn't a care in the world, except that she would have to wait years and years to wear the exquisite gown and slippers.

I looked down at my chipped fingernails that still had dirt in them from that morning when I had dug up carrots and cabbages and squash. I looked down at my unruly hair that now dangled on the floor. It was tangled and dull with dust from the road. I felt my cheeks that were covered in grainy dirt, and now tears.

Roger had been cruel, but had he been right? I knew better than anyone that the years had not been kind to me, but I had never wondered what that unkindness looked like to anyone else. The few people who saw me anymore had seen the change gradually, but to him, to see me after so many years . . . I suddenly saw in my mind what he saw, and I could understand the way he looked at me.

It was Jane, and not me, who the prince had winked and smiled at. I had let myself get so caught up in the idea that the prince had somehow singled me out. He hadn't even noticed me. The foolishness and wounded pride I had felt came rushing back and though no one was there to see me, my cheeks burned.

I fought desperately against the self-pity that was threatening to overtake me because I had learned that once I gave myself permission to feel it, it was like falling into a bottomless pit where I could always find something to be miserable about. I had trained myself from the time I was ten years old that whenever that wave of hopelessness began to creep up on me I had to immediately think of something good so I could pull myself out of that pit; or I had to at least go numb so that I wouldn't have to feel anything at all.

But this time, sitting in a darkening kitchen as I looked over the edge of that pit, I found I didn't have the strength, or even the desire, to pull myself out. I wasn't going to go to the ball. I would feel like a fraud in that dress and fancy slippers. And by not going, I wouldn't have to worry about it anymore. I wouldn't have to struggle with who I was or if I was worthy. I wished I never heard about the ball. Will was right to try to keep it from me, whatever his reasons.

Through eyes blurred with tears, I carefully replaced the lid on the shoes and tied the ribbon. I gently wrapped the dress back in its covering and placed the lid back on the crate and slid it back into the cupboard, covered by pots and pans. The few tears I had shed were already dry and I stood and got to work preparing the evening meal for Victoria and her daughters.

I went back to the front door and retrieved my sack of flour. I wanted to make bread, but I knew I didn't have enough time now. There was no way to know when everyone would be home and they would surely be hungry. Fortunately, there were a few biscuits left over from that morning and some of the berries and butter. I gathered them all up and set them on the table. I then returned to the kitchen and started a fire in the fireplace.

As soon as I felt the warmth from the fire, I realized I was freezing. The thought of leaving the delicious heat sent chills through me, and I couldn't bear to abandon it. I stretched out my weary body on the hearth, not caring about the cinders and soot that clung to me. I untied my shawl, placed it under my head, lay down, and watched the flames dance to a song I couldn't hear.

Chapter 6

As I lay on the hearth, my eyes drooped and I began to dream, or at least I thought I was dreaming. Perhaps it was just a dream of a memory—the memory of when Father had died.

I sat in the wide hall just outside Father's bedroom, waiting for the doctor to come out and tell me Father would be better soon. Victoria, Mabel, Cecelia, and I, as well as what looked like half the village, were waiting for the doctor to emerge. We all feared the time was drawing near; the illness that had taken Father's health so rapidly would soon take his life too.

Will was there too, having loved Henry like a father. His eyes were red, and he tried to hide his face in his hands that were too large for his fourteen-year-old body. It took me a long time to realize that he had been crying. I sat on the cushioned chair, my feet dangling above the floor, my eyes looking straight ahead but seeing nothing.

Everyone stood as the doctor quietly opened the door. Victoria rushed to him, but the doctor softly said, "He wants to see Ella." Victoria's eyes flashed angrily, but she quickly composed herself and returned to her chair.

I stood and walked slowly into the room. I wanted to see Father more than anything, but not like this. Not dying.

The room was dark, lit by only a few candles and a small fire in the fireplace, casting an ominous glow. It was as if the fire knew that death hovered in the air and it refused to give off any more light. I walked slowly toward Father's bed and saw the chair next to the bed, but instead of sitting in it, I used it as a stool to gently climb up onto his bed, careful not to jostle him.

Father's eyes opened slowly and his kind face lit up when he saw me sitting next to him. I looked over to his arm on the other side of his body and found that it rested on a bowl of his own blood.

"Don't worry about that, Pumpkin. It doesn't hurt," he said in a strained whisper. The corners of his eyes crinkled as he smiled, and he reached up his good arm to touch my cheek that was wet with tears.

"Papa, I don't want you to leave me," I whispered. My ten-year-old heart was ready to break.

"Oh, my angel, I don't want to leave you either," Father whispered back. He paused and a faint twinkle lit his eyes. "And do you know what? I never will."

"Really, Papa? You're going to stay?" I covered his hand that rested on my cheek with my own, trying to help him stay with me by holding on to him.

"Not in the way that we're used to. I'll be here, but you won't be able to see me, Ella. You've been my angel your whole life. Now I will get to be yours." Father spoke with a little more vigor, wanting to help me understand. "Sometimes the most important things in our lives are the things we can't see."

"Like what?" I whispered through my tears.

"Like kindness and joy and faith and love. What would we do without those things? Where would we be? They give life meaning."

"What about beauty?" I asked, suddenly remembering our conversation from years before.

Father smiled faintly. "What about it, Pumpkin?"

"You said you can't see beauty in a mirror. Is it like those other things that you can't see, but are important?"

"You are wise beyond your years, Ella. And you have a good memory." He paused to catch his breath. "Yes, Ella. Beauty is like those things. If someone is kind and joyful, faithful and loving, they are beautiful. And beauty will be theirs as long as they keep those qualities a part of who they are." Henry paused again and looked into my eyes . . . Eleanor's eyes. "You are so beautiful." He smiled and closed his own weary eyes. "Ella, choose someone who sees your true beauty." I heard him but didn't completely understand.

"But Papa, how will *I* know what my true beauty is?" I asked.

"You'll know, Ella. You'll know," he whispered.

He lowered his hand wearily from my face, but I grasped it tightly in both of mine on my lap. I thought of how kind these hands were and how much good they had done, how they could create the most beautiful music on his violin that spoke more to the soul than to the ear—hands that not only knew when to serve but how to serve. I looked at his loving face, worn and wrinkled from laughing and crying and thinking and worrying and . . . living. I looked at his gray hair that covered his head and remembered a scripture he used to quote, "The beauty of the old man is in his gray hairs." He used to laugh and say he was becoming more and more beautiful every day.

Father had loved. He had given and worked and sacrificed. He was faithful and charitable and kind.

My father was the most beautiful person I had ever known.

I laid my head on his chest and cried. I felt his hand

gently stroke my hair that cascaded across my back and I heard him whisper, "Take care of them."

I looked up into his face. His eyes were closed. I knew who he was talking about. "I will."

He smiled and nodded as if he already knew what I would say.

"Papa . . . ," I whispered.

With great effort he opened his eyes slowly to look into mine. His eyes seemed so weary, but so peaceful, and even happy.

"I love you," our voices said in unison, mine thick with tears and his weak from clinging to life.

Father's eyes closed as a tender smile touched his lips. "Then it must be true."

I laid my head back down on his chest, and we both slept.

Chapter 7

When I awoke, my body felt stiff and achy. The kitchen was freezing, the heat from the fire having been replaced with empty coldness. I sat up, blinked, and stretched. My eyes were red and swollen from tears I must have shed as I dreamed, but I vowed today I would shed no more. Father would be disappointed in me for moping around. Today was a new day. I would focus my energy on taking care of the home I loved and I would make myself forget about the ball and move on.

I took a deep breath and forced my joints to bend and move. I swung my feet to the floor, rose slowly, and shuffled to the back door, a great yawn overtaking me. The sky was pitch-black, but it didn't feel like night. I knew it was the inky darkness that sucked all the color from the sky in those minutes before the sun arose. And when it did, the sun would splash the world with life and color once again.

I opened the door and went about my normal morning routine of gathering eggs, milking the cow, harvesting whatever was ripe from the garden, and then kneeling for a moment at the two graves at the edge of the garden. When I reached the chicken coop, I was greeted by my little friends,

Mary and Martha. They were always very happy to see me, and though I knew it was because I was the one who fed them, I liked to think they were as fond of me as I was of them.

"Good morning, ladies," I said quietly. I knew no one could hear me, but I still liked to speak softly in the morning. Sprinkling the corn kernels over the dirt, I smiled as I watched the chickens peck and claw at the ground, making sure they got every last one. I always imagined them as funny old women, spending the days gossiping about what was happening at Ashfield.

I stroked them both on their sleek feathers and went over to the barn and found Lucy, waiting for me patiently as always.

"Good morning, girl," I said. I grabbed my bucket from the hook on the wall and sat on my stool next to Lucy. After I rubbed my hands together to warm them, I began the steady work of milking. Resting my head against Lucy's flank, I daydreamed and hummed songs to the rhythm of the milk splashing in the bucket. When I was done milking, I led Lucy out of the barn so she could spend her day grazing in the pasture.

I returned to the kitchen, poured the milk into a clean jug, and took it down to the cellar. I brought up the jug from yesterday's milking and ladled off the cream that had risen to the top of the milk. As soon as I gathered all of the cream, I started a fire, sat down, and got started on churning the cream into butter in my jar and handmade crank. My mouth watered as I imagined spreading the smooth butter on top of a thick slice of warm bread.

Once the butter was thick and creamy, I scooped it into a bowl and put it on the counter, where I kept the last of yesterday's berries in my basket. I ate the few that were left, tightened my shawl around my hair to keep it out of the way, and headed out to the forest with my now empty basket.

I had never been afraid of this forest, or of the little animals that scurried away from me as I approached, or of the owl that watched me with curiosity in the dark gray of early morning. As I picked the berries, I passed the hollow oak tree I used to like to read in when I was a little girl. I smiled as I walked by the boulder I used to climb on and then jump off to try to fly.

The air was crisp and delicious this morning. It had the faint taste of autumn in it that lingered on my tongue and made everything feel clean and exhilarating. The warm heaviness of summer was slowly lifting and the leaves would soon be turning into brilliant versions of themselves. I loved the inevitable and dependable changing of the seasons, and it always put a little skip in my step when they came.

When I reached the pond, I knelt down on the damp grass and splashed water on my face. I gasped a little at the chilliness of the water, but it invigorated me. I started scrubbing under my fingernails and then decided it was no use. I ran my fingers through my long hair and braided it, my arms aching by the time I was done. I stood and let the braid fall to my knees and brushed the dirt off my dress.

As I looked at the glassy smoothness of the pond, I wanted nothing more than to jump all the way in and clean myself from head to foot, but I thought it might be a better idea to take a proper bath at home.

I stepped into the pond, getting the hem of my dress wet, and reached to where the cattails grew and pulled up a few stalks. They were thick and tough and stung my palms. I gathered them into a pile in my arms and then went back to watching the pond and the reflection of the rising sun on it with its accompanying life-giving color.

The snap of a twig behind me didn't even make me jump.

"Good morning, Will," I said pleasantly, still looking at the pond.

"Good morning, Ella," he answered. I turned away from the water and looked at him. His brown hair was falling into his eyes. His skin was darker today than yesterday; he must have worked out in the sun longer than usual, caring for all those horses from the royal procession. He came to stand next to me and smiled down at me.

"So, you mentioned yesterday that I shouldn't worry that you don't have anything to wear to the ball, so I won't," he said with a sly smile. "But have you figured out how you plan on getting there? You don't have a carriage, but I doubt you would want to go on horseback or even cowback, though Lucy loves you enough I'm sure she'd be willing. So, I was wondering if you . . ." Will trailed off when he saw that I wasn't joining in on his joke.

"I'm not going," I replied a little too casually.

"What?" Will asked, totally baffled. "Why aren't you going? I was only joking! You won't have to ride a cow!" He grinned at what I'm sure was the image of me riding up to the palace doors on Lucy. "Isn't this every girl's dream? To be chased after by some ridiculously charming prince and live happily ever after? I'm sorry I kept it from you yesterday, but I really think you need to go."

I sighed, my mood darkening with all of this ball talk. "I am not going and I don't want to talk about it."

The expression on Will's face was a strange combination of confusion and disappointment. "I don't understand."

I could see he wasn't going to back down. "Will, look at me." I held up the corner of my dirty apron. I usually wasn't so filthy, but I hadn't cared much that morning. Besides, my grimy appearance helped prove my point.

Will shook his head in confusion. "What? What's wrong?"

"Do I look like princess material to you?" I meant it as a

rhetorical question, but Will opened his mouth to answer it anyway. I pretended not to notice and continued. "Will, I'm not going to waltz into the palace surrounded by people who are supposed to be there and pretend that I belong. I don't belong anywhere that isn't a barn or a kitchen, and putting on a fancy dress isn't going to change that."

I stopped talking and pursed my lips, surprised at myself for getting so upset, and glanced toward the direction of home.

"I don't want to be late again in case they've decided to become early risers." I smirked a little at the near impossibility of that ever happening. I started for home, but turned back to face him. "Please don't worry about me. It will be all right, Will." I smiled as bravely as I could and spun away from him.

A gentle touch on my wrist stopped my determined steps.

My heart beat strangely as Will's hand slid from my wrist to my hand, and he slowly turned me to face him. He let his hand linger in mine for a moment and then let it fall.

"You have to go to the ball," Will said, unexpectedly fervent.

"Will, I would feel like a fraud. Besides, why would I care about some silly ball when I can barely keep food on the table and my house is falling apart and—"

"That's why you need to go," Will interrupted in a gentle voice. "You need to get away from all of that, even if it's just for a night."

"But what about after the ball is over? Why would I go, only to return to the same problems I had before?"

"Maybe the same problems won't be there," Will stated nonchalantly, but his eyes were impenetrable.

"So if I go to a ball, all my troubles will be over?" I asked sarcastically.

Will sighed. He seemed abruptly torn, yet determined;

the resolve from yesterday returned to his eyes. "You have a chance to get out of here."

I laughed. "Me? Don't be absurd. Why would I go throwing myself at a prince, hoping he'd choose me over a girl who comes from a proper family or who has a dowry, or even a second pair of shoes?" The feelings of self-pity and worthlessness from the night before came flooding back with crushing force, and I ducked my head under the weight of them.

Will suddenly grabbed the tops of my arms, pulling me up to face him. I looked straight back into his eyes, alarmed by his sudden intensity.

"You need to open your eyes and see yourself more clearly," he said. "Don't forget your father and who he was—and who you are."

I tried to jerk out of his grasp at the mention of my father, but he held onto me firmly, not willing to let me go until I understood what he had said. My cheeks flushed and my eyes filled with tears as the spark of anger I felt at Will's words rushed over me. I thought about my father constantly. How dare Will accuse me of forgetting. I almost said those exact words to him, but then stopped myself. I blinked back the tears and my cheeks cooled. I remembered Will's kindness when I felt so alone and the reason behind his words. He was trying to help me in the only way he could. I nodded and managed a small smile.

He was right. Father would have wanted me to go. He wouldn't have wanted me to stay home, feeling sorry for myself and not using the one gift I had left from him.

"I'll think about it," I said finally.

Will studied my face, his hands grasping my arms and holding me close. I felt myself tense, unaccustomed to his closeness, and in response, Will's expression softened and his eyes became less intense, mingled with relief and even tenderness. He looked down at his hands on my arms and slowly released his grip. I exhaled sharply, not realizing I had been holding my breath.

A slow, kind smile brightened Will's face. "He would be proud," he said as he took a deliberate step backward. "And by the way, it doesn't matter how many pairs of shoes you have, Ella. Your plain, black shoes worn out with work and taking care of others are worth more than the queen's dainty slippers any day. And if the prince can't see that, he doesn't deserve you."

Will's smile had an almost imperceptible touch of sadness, and for a small moment I realized that his smiles over the last couple of days had been tinted with that same sorrow. In anyone else, it might not have been noticeable, but Will's smiles had always had been so genuinely happy, and he was always so lighthearted that it was a bit unsettling. Before I could ask him what was wrong, he smiled his old, sincere smile, winked, and walked away.

I shifted the cattails in my arms and picked up my basket of berries, feeling a bit lighter than when I had arrived at the pond. My heartbeat slowly returned to its normal pace once I recovered from Will's uncharacteristic display of intensity and emotion, and I felt relieved that his old smile had returned before he left. And though I was grateful for Will's kind words and the charitable way in which he saw me, I still was not excited about the ball. I was not going to delude myself into thinking I could go to the ball and make the prince fall in love with me—or even notice me at all—and solve all my problems. He hadn't noticed me in town; why would he notice me at the ball?

Chapter 8

When I arrived at home, I was relieved to find that everyone was still asleep. I finished my breakfast preparations and cleared off the dishes from the table that were left there from the night before. Apparently, there would be no repercussions for my not clearing them right away. Another relief. I saw that the food on the dishes was untouched. Victoria, Mabel, and Cecelia must have eaten out last night.

When breakfast was ready, I set about doing my chores. Using the lye I had leached the day before, I made a batch of soothing milk-and-honey soap and an intoxicating rose-water soap. I soaked the cattail stalks I had gathered and used them to weave through the holes in my baskets. After I put my repaired baskets away, I checked on my cheese that was in the process of being pressed and I licked my lips in anticipation. All I had to do was rub it with salt to preserve it and it would last for days. Perhaps we could have some tonight with dinner. I grabbed my worn sapling broom and went through each room, sweeping up the dust and catching any cobwebs.

I hummed as I worked. It was hard labor, but I knew why I did it. It wasn't just because I had been ordered to. It wasn't just because there were no servants to do it anymore. I worked because I loved my home. I loved the satisfaction I felt at the end of a long day when I surveyed my work. My kitchen was spotless, even if it lacked sufficient food and supplies. Every floor shined. There wasn't a cobweb in any corner. The rugs were clean. The curtains were crisp. What furniture we had left was polished and smooth. The beds were made and the linens were fresh. The flowerbeds were filled with beautiful blossoms without a weed in sight.

I knew I had not been born into this house to scrub its floors, wash its windows, or tend its garden. I knew that no one would ever have dreamed I would one day be milking the cow or gathering eggs or cooking over the fire. But I also knew that I would not let it deteriorate just because I hadn't been born to do it. I loved it too much. I loved my father and mother too much. I couldn't do much about the flaking paint on the great pillars that framed the front doors, the roof that needing repairing, or the fence that needed mending. But I did what I could to keep my home the inviting and lovely place it had been for generations before me.

I also worked hard to take care of the people living in the house. When my father had asked me on his deathbed to take care of them, I knew neither of us had any idea what that would someday entail. I had thought that I would simply need to make them feel welcome in the family and our home and their new community. Things had turned out drastically different than my father or I could have ever imagined. Victoria's thirst for power and control had turned my desire to take care of them voluntarily into something that was harshly demanded of me. But it didn't matter. My father was depending on me to take care of them, and whether they would admit it or not, so were they.

I filled up a bucket from the well behind the house and carried it into the kitchen and up the grand staircase to where the bedrooms were. I noiselessly crept into the rooms of Victoria, Mabel, and Cecelia. I quietly filled their water basins and carefully gathered their bed pots, cleaned them out, and returned them to the rooms and then gathered the dirty laundry from off the floor. No one stirred as I busily and silently went about my duties. I then took all the laundry outside to the wash bucket filled with the water I had been boiling in the kettle and began scrubbing the dirty clothes against the washboard.

I was so grateful for the cooler weather today. If I had been sitting doing nothing, I would have been cold, but as I dashed from chore to chore, the coolness was welcome. I refused to think of the long, bitterly cold winter months ahead when I would be forced to stay indoors for most of the time; and when I would have to go outside, the frigid air would make every job that much more difficult. On the other hand, during those long winter months, there was more time to get things done inside that I otherwise wouldn't have time to do.

I also refused to think about the especially harsh winter last year and the empty, gnawing hunger. I wouldn't think about the way my clothes hung off me and how I was too hungry to sleep, and when there was food, almost too hungry to eat. I wouldn't think about how Victoria, Mabel, and Cecelia would leave to eat with friends and come home full and laughing. But there were those other days where there was nowhere to go and we starved together and they glared at me with gaunt, accusing eyes. That was when I had sold Old Gus to buy Lucy, and she had saved us. Her milk became our manna.

I knew that Will remembered last winter, though he never spoke of it, and I suspected that was why he had the preposterous hope that I could somehow win over the prince with my dirty face and chipped fingernails and escape this life of poverty and uncertainty. For now, I would ignore the way the slight chill in the air felt synonymous with starvation, and simply be grateful that I could get so much done without the summer heat draining my energy.

The sun was high in the sky when I was out tending to the garden. My parsnips were growing nicely and I was hopeful that we would have a plentiful crop to use throughout the winter. I was relieved to see that the corn was ready to be harvested. The silk of the ears had turned brown and the kernels spurted their sweet, milky juice when I pressed on them. This meant that I would have more variety in the meals I prepared. Baking only with flour had become monotonous. I had used up the last of the cornmeal I had made from last year's crop months ago and I would need even more corn to feed the chickens through the winter.

I pulled the ears off the stalks and brought them into the house. I hung them up to dry in the warmth of the fire. Soon, I would grind the kernels into meal for corn bread. I had a much better and larger crop than last year and felt optimistic that we would be able to eat well this winter.

As I hung up the last ear of corn, I heard the sound of muted voices coming from the dining room. Victoria and her daughters had slept later than usual, but it certainly was not the latest they'd ever slept. I could hear an unusual hum of excitement in the tone of their voices as I walked closer to the dining room.

I entered the room, unacknowledged by the women eating there, and stood in my usual corner and waited for them to be finished. It was such a terrible waste of time, just standing there when I had so many other things to do, but I dared not defy Victoria by doing anything other than what she had ordered me to do.

"I'm going to wear my pink gown with the swooping sleeves," Mabel said, stuffing a handful of berries in her mouth.

"I'm going to wear my . . ." Cecelia's words became unintelligible as she spoke with her mouth too full and crumbs flew out of her mouth.

"You're not wearing either of those dresses!" snapped Victoria. "We must find you something so extraordinary that the prince will notice *no one* but you." I wasn't looking directly at Victoria so I could have imagined it, but I thought I saw her eyes shoot me a vicious look.

"Me?" they both replied, gesturing to themselves.

"Either one," Victoria said, shrugging her shoulders and waving a careless hand in the air.

I looked at Victoria for the first time that morning and barely contained a gasp. Victoria's eyes had dark circles underneath them and they were even more sunken than the day before. She often looked haggard after being up late and sleeping half the day away, but this was a new level of hideousness.

I glanced down at Victoria's plate and saw that her food was untouched. I normally would have worried that my cooking had been unsatisfactory to Victoria and that there would be a punishment in conjunction with that, but Mabel and Cecelia were stuffing their faces as if it were the most delicious meal they had ever had. It was undeniable what was going on.

Victoria was ill. Very ill.

I listened to the conversation to hear if either of the girls would inquire after their mother's health or even take notice that she looked like she had lost ten pounds in a week, but the only topic was the ball and what they would wear and how beautiful they would look.

Mabel and Cecelia were very pretty girls—if you had just met them. They both had long, glistening mahogany hair, lovely features, large brown eyes, and rosy cheeks. They had been trained to carry themselves with an air of dignity and refinement. But they had a whining quality to their voices that made everything they said sound empty and foolish. Their brown eyes could have been soft and warm if they hadn't had the look of haughtiness and blankness about them. Their straight backs and smooth manners could have been seen as confidence and grace but instead it came off as arrogance and coldness.

The three women never stopped talking as they finished their food and left the room. I quickly cleared the table, ran upstairs to help them dress, and then returned downstairs to finish cleaning up breakfast. I took the food from Victoria's untouched plate to save for later. As I began scrubbing the soot off the hearth, Victoria and her daughters looked through their wardrobes for some new ideas on what they would wear to the ball.

The rare sound of carriage wheels in the front yard distracted me from my work. I dropped my scrubbing brush, wiped my hands on a clean, damp rag, hurried to the front door, and opened it to see who could be calling. Nobody ever came to Ashfield any more. Victoria and her daughters usually preferred to be entertained than to entertain. Besides, they were so embarrassed by the state of the house that they never invited anyone anyway.

I poked my head out the door and then flung it open and dashed to the carriage as soon as the driver opened the door and Jane stepped out. I opened my arms to embrace my friend, so excited that she had finally come to visit, but as I came close, she abruptly held her hands out to stop me.

"Ella! What is all over your dress?" Jane cried. Her nose wrinkled in disgust, and she kept her hands up as if warning me to stay back.

I looked down and realized I was covered with dirt from working in the garden and cinder from scrubbing the hearth. My hair had escaped my long braid in some places and framed my face wildly. But my hands were clean, so I grasped Jane's hands instead.

"Really, Ella. What have you been doing with yourself?" Jane said as she slowly pulled her hands out of mine.

I carefully brushed my hands against my dress and blushed. In my enthusiasm at seeing Jane, I had forgotten what I looked like. And though I had worn the same dress the day before, it had been a bit cleaner and so today it was unrecognizable. The way she looked at me simply reinforced the fact that I had no business going to any ball.

I didn't know what to say. I was afraid that if I told Jane that I was so dirty because I had been scrubbing, dusting, churning, milking, and gardening, it would get back to Victoria and I would be punished for letting Jane know what I did around the house. As far as anyone else was concerned, things were just as they always had been at Ashfield. I thought about lying to Jane, perhaps saying I had slipped and fallen into some mud, but I just decided to stay silent.

Jane changed the subject when I didn't answer. "Oh, Ella! I had such a wonderful time with your sisters last night! I do so wish you could have stayed. They all came to my house and we laughed and talked for hours! We're all going to do our hair the same for the ball. Won't that be fun?" Jane made her way toward the front steps. "You've never told me how charming your sisters were. And your mother! What a divine woman she is!"

I listened to Jane in silence as I followed her up the porch steps and through the front door I had left open in my excitement. When we reached the foyer, I saw Jane survey the empty room with a bewildered expression on her face. The last time she had been in this house, there had been sofas, end tables, rugs, vases filled with flowers. . . . I wrung my hands uncomfortably and looked up to see Cecelia and Mabel standing a little stunned at the top of the stairs. Apparently, this visit was unexpected. It seemed that they had played their new best friend roles so well that Jane felt comfortable enough to drop by unannounced.

Mabel and Cecelia quickly recovered from their shock. They came running down the stairs and leapt joyously into the arms of their newest friend. Just as I had the day before when I saw them talking together in the town square, I thought it strange that the girls had just now decided to become friends, though they had lived in the same village for half their lives. I was sure that whatever the reason was, it involved Mabel and Cecelia getting something out of it. And I couldn't ignore the fact that there just happened to be a ball coming up and Jane had lots of pretty things that she would gladly share with her friends.

Their conversation from the night before continued where it had left off. I watched in dazed silence as the three friends ascended the staircase, Jane with her arms linked through an arm of the other two. Mabel and Cecelia seemed determined to occupy Jane's attention and it worked. None of them looked back at me.

"Thank you for letting us use your driver and carriage last night. Our driver has been ill and our carriage has a broken wheel," Cecelia said.

"Oh, and please excuse the state of the house. We're redecorating," said Mabel as they disappeared into the third bedroom at the top of the stairs.

As I listened to their lies, a thought crossed my mind. I knew that I looked different than I usually did when I was around Jane, but she had changed too, even since yesterday. She looked at me the way my stepsisters did; the way Roger did; the way Victoria did—with revulsion. I remembered that Roger had called me mad. It made me cringe thinking of the things Victoria said about me when I wasn't around, and what she had possibly told Jane when they dined with her last night.

I couldn't pull my gaze away from the bedroom door for a long time. When my eyes finally obeyed me, they dropped to stare at the freshly polished floor beneath my feet and I saw my distorted reflection in the perfectly cut stones.

I felt moisture pricking behind my eyes, but I had vowed there would be no tears today.

Chapter 9

I HID MYSELF AWAY IN THE KITCHEN FOR MOST OF THE DAY. After I folded the dry laundry, I made a pile of clothes in the corner that needed to be mended. I finally had time to make bread and enough flour to make a couple of loaves. I bent over the table and comforted myself with the familiar rhythm of kneading the dough. Fold, push, turn. Fold, push, turn. I kneaded until the dough was smooth and rising slightly around my hands. Then I put the loaves in bread pans and put them on the hearth in front of the fire, rotating them every once in a while so they could brown on all sides. The aroma was heavenly and heartening. In between rotations, I fed Mary and Martha again. They were eating more now that the weather was cooling. The pit of my stomach felt cold for a moment.

It was late afternoon when I heard footsteps approaching the kitchen. There were so many unusual sounds today and it was making me feel on edge. With a gasp, I realized it must be Jane since no one who lived in this house ever came to the kitchen willingly. Victoria would not want Jane to see me working in the kitchen, sewing the top button on Cecelia's blue chiffon dress, but I thought of it too late for me to hide and the footsteps came to a halt at the arched entrance of the kitchen.

I looked up from my sewing to see Victoria towering in the open doorway. I rose so quickly that the dress fell onto the floor, dangerously close to the flickering fire. I was relieved that I had just cleaned the hearth or I would have had to figure out a way to get cinder out of chiffon. I didn't know if I should bend to pick the dress up, but I didn't want to look away from Victoria. In my moment of hesitation, Victoria began talking and so I listened.

"Your friend Jane is going to stay for dinner." She seemed to be pleased with the idea that her daughters had taken my only friend. Reminding me that Jane was *my* friend was just a small way of hurting me. "We will have chicken."

Victoria rarely made requests for dinner; it would require her to actually talk to me. I prided myself on becoming an adequate cook with minimal training, and whatever I made, even when ingredients were scarce, seemed to please the people who ate it. We rarely ate meat because it was too expensive or because we didn't have any animals we could spare for such a luxury. Victoria obviously didn't want Jane to think we were starving or close to it.

I never argued with Victoria, but her request was preposterous.

"Stepmother, we only have two chickens left. They each usually lay only one egg a day. If we only have one chicken, we won't have enough eggs to eat and cook with." *We already don't,* I silently added. My palms were sweating and I was shaking. I tried to be persuasive but respectable, pleading but not whining. I saw no budging in Victoria's expression but I was desperate for her to change her mind.

Victoria's sunken eyes tightened, and she clenched her frail jaw. "You heard me," she whispered viciously. I nodded and ducked my head and Victoria turned to leave the room. But as she passed the doorway, her hand reached out to touch the wall and she turned back around. Her gaze swept past me and into the kitchen, and she stood silently for a moment as she took in every corner.

She looked back at me. "I haven't forgotten about your little secret," she warned. She tried to spin away from me and stride out of the room dramatically, but she was too weak and feeble for the actions to have their usual flare.

I stood in silence and forced my breathing to slow. I had almost forgotten that she had seen the fear in my eyes when she mentioned that she had been in the kitchen the day before. But I wouldn't let myself overreact. She didn't even know what she was looking for. It was almost as if she was challenging me to do something about it so that she could catch me, and I wasn't going to give in. Right now, the more important problem was food—as usual.

It certainly was not the first time I would have to kill one of the chickens. I knew that's what they were there for. They provided food in the form of eggs, but they were also food themselves. It had never bothered me before and I had even looked forward to the times that it would be necessary to kill one to eat for an especially delicious dinner when one of the chickens was getting older. And there had usually been enough to spare.

But now that there were only two of them left, they had become two of the few friends I had in my little world. I rebuked myself for becoming attached to the chickens when I knew they wouldn't and couldn't live forever. I knew better than to let myself feel, knowing that with feeling came hurting.

Both chickens were healthy, but Martha was older. She seemed like the logical choice, but I couldn't see the logic this time. I was too emotionally invested and had even come to rely on my little friends to greet me every morning. I had raised both of them from the time they were chicks, and they trusted me.

I rubbed my fingers on my temples and tried to push the thought out of my mind. Chickens don't trust. They eat and sleep and lay eggs. They don't love. They just survive. I kept repeating that. I had to do what was necessary, and it was better for Martha to die this way than to get old and sick anyway, I told myself.

I picked up Mabel's dress from off the floor, draped it over the chair, and opened the kitchen door. I walked to the barn and grabbed the axe that hung on the wall and trudged over to the chicken coop. Mary and Martha were both asleep in the henhouse, but they awakened at the sound of my footsteps. I tried not to think about how happy it made me when they would come to greet me excitedly. I tried not to think about how lonely Mary would feel without her older friend to keep her company.

My sorrow abruptly turned from Martha's fate to Mary's. I had been so sad for Martha, knowing her life was about to end and that I was going to have to be the one to end it. But what about Mary? What was she going to do without Martha? I thought of Jane giggling and trying on dresses with Mabel and Cecelia and suddenly realized I knew what it felt like to lose a friend. I reached out and gently smoothed the feathers on the back of Mary's neck.

I broke my promise to myself and finally allowed the tears to spill over. It was like they had been waiting to be set free all day, and it was worse than if I had let them escape a little bit at a time. The sobs choked me and I knelt down in the dirt and let them come.

"It will be all right, Mary. I'm here," I whispered hoarsely.

I turned my tear-filled eyes on Martha and gently picked her up out of the coop. I stroked the fluffy smoothness of her back and kissed the top of her head. My tears bathed her feathers and I carried her to the chopping block.

***

IT WAS COMPLETELY DARK WHEN I FOUND MYSELF SITTING beside the pond. I rarely ever came to the pond twice in one day, but I had nowhere else to go. I had discreetly prepared and left the meal of chicken and dumplings on the table, knowing there would be terrible consequences if Jane had seen me serving them their meal and standing in my usual corner, waiting to clear off their dirty dishes. Besides, I didn't want to see anybody anyway. And I especially didn't want to watch them enjoy their particularly delectable dinner.

Jane seemed to be utterly taken in by the consummate acting abilities of my stepmother and stepsisters, and I knew I couldn't blame her. I knew how charming they could be when they wanted to be, when they wanted something. Jane was naive and sincere and probably thought they truly wanted to be her friends.

In a way, I felt sorry for Jane. She had never known anyone who could use her so callously, so she would never suspect anything like this of her new friends. But there was another part of me that couldn't ignore the fact that in the past ten years Jane had never come to visit me to giggle and talk and try on pretty clothes, not that I would have had the time or had been allowed to, and not that I had any dresses to share anyway; but I had always just assumed that our friendship was too real for those other things, that we simply enjoyed each other's company. But Jane seemed to be thoroughly enjoying herself this afternoon with her new friends.

The feeling of loneliness consumed me.

The first hints of self-pity were stirring again and I fought against them with what little strength I had left in me. I shook off the minor betrayal of Jane and the fact that

I had lost, or at least had to share, my only friend. But then I thought of something. If Jane hadn't even known what my life was truly like, had she ever really been a friend at all? Or, if she had known, would she even want me as a friend?

The loneliness consumed and then crushed.

I hugged my knees up to my chest and buried my face in my arms . . . and waited.

When I decided it was safe to return to the house, I left the seclusion of the pond and walked home. I saw that Jane's carriage had gone and I entered the house through the servants' entrance—my entrance. Everyone's voices were upstairs. I wouldn't have to worry about them any more tonight.

I went back outside and milked Lucy again and fed Mary her dinner of corn. I tried to comfort myself by thinking that the corn would last that much longer with only one chicken left. Still, I vowed that one day Mary would be surrounded by plenty of friends to gossip the day away with. I stroked Mary's smooth back and was pleased that she didn't seem the least bit concerned about the day's events, and was perhaps delighted that she got a little extra dinner that night. I smiled and wondered what life was really like for this pleasant little chicken pecking away at her corn. Did she ever want to live a different life? Was she content where she was, or did she ever wonder if there was more out there? I laughed at myself and my ridiculous, unanswerable, trivial questions. It had been a very long day and I must be exhausted.

I returned to the house and cleared the table and washed the dishes. I felt slightly ashamed for being a tiny bit grateful that Victoria was not feeling well, but I had gotten away with not clearing the table immediately after dinner for two nights in a row.

I filled a bucket with water from the well and brought it into the warm kitchen, sloshing water all over the place, and closed the door behind me. Tomorrow would be Sunday and I had to wash my dress, and myself, before morning. I pulled off my dress and took a sponge bath next to the fire. The water was cold, but cold water got me just as clean as warm, and it was faster.

I scrubbed my hair and body with the milk and honey soap I made, and scrubbed under my fingernails, finally ridding them of the dirt from the garden that had been there for days. Once I was clean, I put on my worn nightgown. I combed through my hair and wove it until it fell in a damp braid all the way down my back and to my knees, chilling me through the thin fabric.

I sat down on my chair in front of the fire in the kitchen and carefully mended any rips or holes I had put in my dress that week. The seam was coming loose in the back and I tightened it up. The hem was beginning to unravel in one spot and I stitched it. The most difficult part was getting the cinder, soot, and dirt out of the fabric. I had to scrub hard enough to get the stains out, but not so hard that I damaged the already worn material. I hung the dress on the line with the ears of corn to dry by the fire, and made the long climb up to my room.

My room was in the tallest tower on the east corner of Ashfield. Though it may have appeared to be a prison, it was actually my only real sanctuary in the house. I loved the tranquility and how I could see the woods and the pond out of the east window; and out of the west window, I could see the palace. Both views were breathtaking in their own way.

The east tower had not always been my bedroom. After Father died, I had run up to this tower and refused to come out. Grace had begged me to come down and eat, and the rest of the servants had tried to lure me down with promises of treats and presents. When I had still refused to come down, my belongings had gradually been moved up to the east tower where they would stay. Fortunately for me, Victoria had not objected to my moving to the tower, and I think she even preferred it.

I simply could not stand being in the house without my own father and mother there with me. I had never actually known my mother, but to live in the house with three strangers instead of either one of my parents was unbearable. And they were not just strangers—they were cruel strangers who immediately took over the house and started callously ordering everyone around. It wasn't long before I, too, was ordered around, much to the dismay and even outrage of our servants. But, like me, they were completely powerless against Victoria.

Feeling clean, yet slightly lethargic, I slowly made my way across the house and up to my tower. It seemed that everyone had gone to bed and the house was dark and peaceful. I didn't bother to light a candle as I climbed up the tall, dark stairs. I opened the door at the top and took a moment to look out the west window that overlooked the palace.

I felt a flurry of butterflies in my stomach when I imagined again that I could possibly be entering the palace gates in less than a week's time. Why had I told Will I would consider going? Who did I think I was, thinking I could go to the ball? But, if I was being honest with myself, I knew I would regret it forever if I didn't go. And fortunately—miraculously—I had something I could wear. It was easier now that I was clean to consider the possibility that perhaps putting on my beautiful gown and slippers would help make me feel a little less ridiculous walking into the palace.

I sighed and walked over to look out the east window. The smoke from Will's chimney was floating over the trees. I smiled to myself, amazed at how easily he was able to persuade me to consider going to the ball when I had been absolutely against the idea. He had made me open my eyes when I hadn't realized they had been closed. And as much as I thought about Father, I truly hadn't considered the fact that he would want me to go, that he certainly wouldn't have thought I was unworthy to walk through the palace doors with my head held high.

I left the window, laid my aching body down on the blanket on the floor, and fell into a deep sleep.

Chapter 10

On Sunday morning I did all my chores, including boiling water and drawing baths for Mabel and Cecelia and dressing them in their Sunday dresses. Once I was ready for church in my crisp, clean, mended dress, I went to see if Victoria was going to wake up in time to come with us. Victoria was still in bed and told us to go without her. I couldn't remember the last time she hadn't gone to church. She wasn't exactly religious, but she was very social and she hated to miss any kind of gathering. I brought her up some water and some berries and bread on a tray, but she pushed them away and told me to leave.

I sat in our usual spot on a side pew near the back of the chapel, but my stepsisters walked past me to sit in the middle. I wasn't particularly wounded. It was a small relief not to have to play the role of happy family. I watched as the congregation filed into the small chapel. As always, when I saw Mrs. Thatcher come in, I was filled with one of my fondest memories of Father.

When I was about seven years old, I was awakened from a deep sleep by a large hand vigorously shaking my shoulder.

"Wake up, Ella," Father whispered urgently. "Mrs.

Thatcher is sick, and we must go and help their family." I opened my heavy eyelids, but he had already left the room.

I sat up, rubbed my eyes, and pushed my warm quilts off me. The floor was chilly and I shivered as I dressed quickly in the darkness. I ran down the stairs and out the front door. The frosty morning air filled my lungs and forced my weary eyes to open the rest of the way. I ran to the carriage that was waiting in the front drive, and Father held out his hand to help me up. I was surprised to see the village doctor sitting next to Father, along with Grace, and another woman sitting on the bench opposite. The only place for me to sit was on Father's lap and he was already holding his arms out for me. I climbed onto his lap and rested my head on his shoulder.

"Good morning, Grace," I said politely, though my curiosity burned. I was surprised to see my governess there. Not because she hadn't helped me dress that morning, but because she had her packed bag sitting on her lap.

Father answered my unasked question. "Grace is going to help the Thatcher children. Their mother is very ill and the boys need some looking after."

I nodded and my gaze shifted from Father to the doctor and I smiled up at him. My father had told me once that he was the doctor who had tried to keep my mother alive. I knew him as the one who treated me when I had the measles when I was five. He was a kind, gentle man. He was the most like Father of anyone I knew, which was probably why they were such good friends. He returned my smile and then turned to look out the window. I watched him as his smile disappeared and his hands began to wring on his lap.

I waited for someone to tell me who the other woman was next to Grace, but they all seemed too preoccupied. I was glad to share my governess and help in that small way, but I still didn't know why I was going. I barely knew the

Thatcher family, and I felt I was too young to help in any real way.

When we arrived at the Thatcher's little cottage, I could hear the rowdy boys running around inside the house, even at that early hour. Father knocked on the door and the oldest boy answered and let us in, then ran back to playing with his brothers. The small house was in complete disarray, and the boys were running around playing some sort of game that involved swords and fighting and dying, then jumping up and starting it all over again. Father and the doctor walked to the back room, and I followed while Grace masterfully worked on settling the boys down.

There was a small sound coming from the back room where we were walking. I recognized it as the soft wail of a newborn baby. We reached the last door and the doctor knocked on it softly. There was no answer, but he opened the door slowly and we followed him in. My eyes followed the sounds of the crying baby and saw that he was nestled next to his mother on the bed, wrapped in a faded blue blanket. His tiny fists were clenched; one fist was in his mouth and he was obviously looking for some way to ease his hunger. My chin trembled looking at the poor, tiny thing, and I wondered why no one was helping him. I was just about to go over to him, when the unnamed woman who had ridden there with us walked past me and gently and expertly picked up the whimpering baby.

She swiftly left the room, and I looked after her. I turned my face up to ask Father what was happening, but he was staring at the bed. Mr. Thatcher was kneeling next to the bed, holding his wife's frail hand. She was so pale her face blended in with the whiteness of the pillow that cradled her head. Her dark hair stuck to her face, sticky with sweat, and though she was covered with heavy quilts, she shivered and quietly moaned.

I pulled my eyes away from the tragic scene on the bed and back to Father's face and saw a tear running down his cheek. I placed my hand in his strong one, trying to figure out why he was so affected by what he saw. I looked back to the scene on the bed and realized that what he saw in front of him was like looking into a mirror, only seven years earlier. His heart was breaking for this little family, knowing the pain they were experiencing.

Father nodded to the doctor and quietly left the room so that the doctor could do his work. We walked down the narrow hall. As we passed one of the small bedrooms, I saw the unnamed woman sitting on a wooden rocking chair, feeding the tiny baby. His wails had stopped and his little tummy was finally full, probably for the first time since he'd been born. I realized this woman was an angel, quietly doing what needed to be done, and saving this baby's life in the process. For the first time, I realized that someone must have once done that for me.

When Father and I returned to the room, Grace miraculously had the boys all seated on the worn wooden bench and was telling them a story about dragons and knights. Father told me to wait inside while he went out to get something. He and the driver returned carrying one basket in each of their hands filled to overflowing with food, blankets, clothes, and toys for the boys. Father gave a basket to me and asked me to hand out the toys to each child.

I marveled at their delight with the presents and their joy at the food, and I felt that same delight and joy at being a part of lightening others' burdens. I realized that our cooks must have been up all night preparing all of this delicious food. The bread was still warm, as well as the ham and syrup. This had been a great effort by many people, and my father had been the orchestrator of it.

That was why Father had brought me—to learn to be

aware of someone else's suffering and what it felt like to help ease that suffering.

He could have left me in bed. I could have been sleeping, safe and warm in my feather bed covered in fluffy quilts, a hot breakfast waiting for me. He could have gone alone and told me about it later, but I doubted he would have. How many times had he done something like this for others and had said nothing?

My thoughts returned to the present, and I waved and smiled at Mrs. Thatcher, who was radiant and healthy. She smiled back, her soft, brown eyes crinkling a bit at the corners and her graying hair catching the light streaming in from the window. She was unable to wave because she was holding yet another small boy—her first grandchild—but her eyes still held profound gratitude for kindness from years before.

After the opening hymn, Mr. Grey took his place at the podium. He was a jovial sort of man and his sermons almost always filled me with hope and encouragement. But today, at the first words out of his mouth, my mood dampened.

"Welcome. I know that you are all very excited about the prince's announcement the other day about the ball." I tried not to irreverently roll my eyes. "But I am grateful to see so many of you still found time out of your busy planning and dress-making to attend church this lovely day." He beamed down at us and the congregation chuckled. A few young ladies sighed, indicating what a hardship it truly was.

His sermon continued and, thankfully, all talk of balls and princes seemed to be over. There was a tangible excitement in the air, obviously having to do with the ball. But there was something else besides excitement. Tension absolutely filled the room—tension so thick it was blinding. I couldn't help occasionally glancing around at the people sitting near me.

Will sat with some other young men who also worked in the king's stables. They were all muscular boys, used to the vigorous tasks they had to perform day in and day out. Will was older than the other boys by a few years. I only knew a few of them besides Will, but they were certainly popular among the young ladies. The girls my age were usually trying to sneak little glimpses at them when their mothers weren't watching, or passing them love notes. But today, there wasn't any of that.

I looked, only moving my eyes, at the girls my age who were seated with their families on the pews. Today they weren't trying to get the boys' attention at all; they were eyeing each other with open hostility. I was appalled, but not surprised, to see that the most hostile were my stepsisters. I was immediately intimidated at the thought of competing with any of these girls, who looked as if they would stop at nothing to win over the prince, and I wanted no part of it. Not only because I knew I would lose, but because I didn't think I would even survive the battle.

I caught the eye of Roger Wallace and looked away quickly. It took an incredible amount of self-control to stifle the laugh that was threatening to escape me. It was certainly not because he had elicited any kind of warmth or coyness from me. It was because even poor Roger Wallace was being ignored today, and he had an unmistakable, unintentionally comical, scowl on his face.

***

When the service was over, I usually would have gone to talk and catch up with a few friends and neighbors. But I barely talked to anyone today. Most of the girls my age had gone straight home, without bothering to say good-bye. Mr. Grey came to me and inquired after my family. I mentioned that Victoria had been too ill to come to church that morning, and he got a little pucker between his eyebrows.

"Well, give that sweet lady my best and let me know if you need anything, my dear," he said, patting my shoulder soothingly.

"I will. Thank you, Mr. Grey."

I turned around and noticed that Mabel and Cecelia had gone to talk to Jane on the lawn in front of the chapel. I raised my hand to wave to Jane, but she must not have seen because she didn't wave back. I quickly put my arm back down by my side in embarrassment. I wasn't eager to return home alone to face Victoria and whatever temper she was in, but I was also not in the mood to be ignored, whether it was on purpose or not. I pursed my lips and strode off in the direction of home.

I heard footsteps and saw that Will had caught up to me. He walked casually with his hands in his pockets. "How did you like the service today?" I heard a smile in his voice.

I blushed a little in embarrassment. I hadn't been paying very close attention. "Did you notice the girls acting strangely today?" I asked, casually changing the subject.

"I don't notice any of those girls," he teased.

I smiled. "Of course you don't," I said sarcastically. "I've never seen anything like that. It was like there was a war going on right in the middle of church, but the weapons were glares and squinty eyes." It seemed a little silly now and I laughed softly.

Will chuckled. "I don't envy you, you know. Women fight a harder battle than I'll ever know."

"I don't know about that," I said, thinking about the scowl on Roger Wallace's face. "We're all competing *for* the prince; it must be at least that difficult for the men to be competing *with* the prince." I didn't think before I spoke and didn't realize how awkward it would be for Will to reply. I didn't mean to imply that he personally was competing, but just that the announcement of the ball had affected everyone, not just the women.

When Will didn't answer immediately, I looked over at him, ready to explain what I meant. When I saw the blank look on his face, I realized for the first time that he could actually be jealous of the prince over some girl and I got a terrible feeling in the pit of my stomach. But I pushed it away. Just because he helped me and was my friend didn't mean I had any claim on him, I reminded myself. I only saw him in the mornings when we met at the pond. I didn't know how many parties and dances he went to, or how many admirers he had. Judging by the way the girls acted around him, I guessed it was not a small few.

He was staring straight ahead, looking suddenly serious. "There's no competition," he mumbled. I started to argue with him, but he went on. "So, you're saying 'we' now? Do you include yourself in that group of women fighting for the prince?" he asked with a shrewd grin.

I sighed but couldn't help smiling at his expression. "I told you I would think about it. I know Father would want me to go, and if I do go, it would only be because I don't want to regret it later. I just want to see what it's like. But I am not willing, nor am I worthy, to compete with those girls," I said.

I pictured my gown and slippers and the thought of putting them on with my dirty hands, chipped nails, and ugly calluses made me cringe.

"Ella! You're worth one hundred—" Will began.

"Will, there's no competition," I said with a grin, and he rolled his eyes.

We walked the rest of the way in silence, both thinking our own thoughts, until we reached Ashfield. I knew every curve of the road that led home but was still surprised to find that we had already arrived. I sighed and looked at the home I loved. I had dedicated my whole life to keeping the house as grand as it once was. I had to admit I was doing a decent job, considering the enormity of that task and the trials that came along with it. I felt a sense of pride whenever I looked at Ashfield long enough to enjoy it.

I suspected my ancestors might not be completely satisfied with the overall condition of the house and property now, but I hoped that they would be proud of my efforts to keep it beautiful. It was my unconventional way of honoring them.

I turned to look at Will to thank him for walking me home, but I was taken aback by his gentle expression. He took a step closer to me. "You are a beautiful person, Ella. Do you know that? You give and give with no thought of getting. You work hard without complaint and you see the good in difficult circumstances." He smiled. "I've only known one other person like that in my life."

We both knew who he was talking about—Henry Blakeley. I blinked my suddenly tear-filled eyes and whispered, "Thank you."

Will took another step closer to me, so close I could see how the sunlight had lightened the tips of his eyelashes. Then in a gesture that surprised me by its tenderness and unexpectedness, he hesitatingly raised his hand, browned from the sun and roughened from work, gently brushed my hair back from my face, and rested it against my burning cheek.

Chapter 11

WILL SUDDENLY SMILED, DROPPED HIS HAND, AND CONtinued on toward his home, leaving me standing in the road alone. I stood there for a moment and then continued to the house, tripping over a rock I didn't see. Once inside, I slipped my shoes off. Before I went to the kitchen to prepare lunch, I went to see how Victoria was feeling. I was genuinely beginning to worry about her. I knocked softly on the door and heard a weak, monotone voice mutter, "Enter."

I opened the door and saw that all the curtains were still closed. The room was dank and utterly black. I stood and waited for my eyes to adjust.

"Would you like me to open the drapes?" I asked.

"No," Victoria replied in a hoarse whisper.

"Can I do anything for you?" My hands began to tremble. I still couldn't see Victoria, though I could make out the shape of her large bed against the opposite wall.

I heard a rustling of sheets and saw Victoria's eyes shining in the darkness from the bed. I could tell just from the glare of them that her eyes were tight slits.

"Do you know what you can do for me?" she asked. She held up something light that shimmered even in the darkness. I couldn't breathe. My heart stopped beating for a moment and then pounded so hard it felt like it was trying to escape or punish me. "You can tell me why you've been hiding this gown and these slippers while we have been starving to death."

The walls blurred around me for a moment, and I swayed on my feet as the wave of dread overtook me.

"I told you that you couldn't hide anything from me. If you were able to control your fear, perhaps I never would have discovered these, but you gave your little secret away." She pushed herself more upright on her pillows. "First thing tomorrow, you will take these things into town. They are worth more than enough to buy new ball gowns for my girls and me."

I stood motionless. The blood was pounding so violently in my ears that I could barely understand her words, and I shook my head to keep the room from spinning. I couldn't make sense of the image in front of me—Victoria sitting on her bed, my precious things in her vile hands. I swallowed back the lump in my throat and blinked back the hot tears.

"One more thing," she said. She reached into the drawer on her nightstand and pulled out the long thin stick that was used for the sole purpose of whipping my hands. "For your deceit." Numbly, I moved forward, shocked that my knees didn't buckle. I wanted to resist. I wanted to run from the room or even tell her she had no right to my things, but submitting to her control had become a habit that I had never been able to break. My fear of her, I realized, had grown instead of dwindled over the years. When Victoria demanded something of me, I instantly became the frightened child who had been left alone in an unfamiliar world. I reached the side of her bed and held out my hands obediently, and she whipped my palms that hadn't yet healed.

After nine lashings, Victoria raised her arm for what I

hoped would be the last one. Suddenly, her eyes rolled back, her head hit the pillow, and the stick dropped out of her hands. I gasped and realized she had fainted. I slapped her cheeks gently with the backs of my fingers and called out her name. I dipped my hands in the water basin, washing the blood off my palms, and wiped Victoria's clammy forehead. It was no use. She needed the doctor.

As I turned to dash out of the room, I paused. I looked back at my beautiful gown and slippers sitting on the bed next to Victoria and refused to leave them. I mustered all the courage I could, ran back to the bed, snatched them up, and ran them up to my tower. I pulled up three loose floorboards and quickly and carefully put my dress and slippers into the hollow underneath. I replaced the floorboards, giving myself slivers in my haste, and dashed back down the stairs.

Breathless and sweating, I ran back past Victoria's room and saw that she was still unconscious. I flew down the stairs and opened the front door, slamming right into Cecelia and Mabel. Their faces turned from shock to fury in an instant. They opened their mouths to berate me, but I spoke first.

"Run and get the doctor!" I ordered.

I had never in my life told my stepsisters to do anything, and they stood there on the porch in astonishment. I gaped at them for a moment until I realized they were not going to move, not even blink. I groaned in frustration and ran past them.

"Go help your mother," I yelled over my shoulder. I didn't turn back to see if they had obeyed.

I ran as fast as I could to the main road and didn't stop until I reached the doctor's house. I pounded on the door and told him that Victoria was ill the moment it opened.

He grabbed his bag and ran to his carriage, and I followed him. He turned around and looked at me. "You look like you need to rest. Stay here for a while and have the maid get you some cookies and tea." He drove off before I could protest.

It had been years since I had had cookies, but they had never sounded less appetizing to me. I had no intention of going into the doctor's house and resting. I waited until he turned the corner and I began walking back home, grateful that I could take some time to catch my breath and calm my frantic heart and grasp what had happened.

Victoria had found out my secret. After years of hiding them, she had found my gown and slippers and had ordered me to sell them. And I knew that the only reason she wasn't taking them herself, besides the fact that it was Sunday, was that she was too weak. I sighed, again feeling guilty for being relieved that she didn't feel well and that I was able to hide my things away from her once more. But now that she knew about them and that I was adding open rebellion to my deceit, I would surely pay for this.

I walked with my head down, watching as my toes on each foot took turns peeking out from under my hem as I walked. The sound of a carriage approaching made me lift my eyes. Carefree laughter drifted over the countryside as what I recognized as a royal carriage came toward me from the opposite direction. I looked into the faces of its occupants, and my heart stopped as the prince's eyes met mine.

His laughter stopped abruptly, and he stared back at me with an expression that looked something like concern mingled with bewilderment. I curtsied respectfully as the carriage hurried past me, and I was caught in the cloud of dust left behind it. My curiosity pulled my gaze back toward the carriage, and I saw that the prince had turned around in his seat to look at me. His gaze was so intense, I thought for a moment that he was going to stop and talk to me. My stomach filled with butterflies and dread at the same time.

It would be incredible to be able to talk to the prince, but I would have no idea what to say, and besides that, I couldn't begin to imagine what I looked like. I bit my lip nervously, but the carriage never slowed. He simply watched me until they disappeared around the bend. I couldn't tell if I felt relief or disappointment once he was gone.

I continued walking toward home, covered in dust and sweat, and tried to imagine what I must have looked like to the prince, and what made him stare at me that way. Did he know that it had been me who had stood ten feet away from him when he announced the ball? That I was the girl next to Jane?

By the time I arrived at home, Victoria had been revived with some smelling salts and had fallen back to sleep. The doctor and I stayed up all night watching over her and changing the cloths on her forehead. I wasn't sure if the doctor usually stayed to perform such menial tasks, or if he wanted to stay and help me when he realized I would be doing it alone. He kept glancing over his shoulder. I assumed he was waiting for my stepsisters to come and help their mother. After a while, he stopped looking.

Victoria never fully regained consciousness until the morning. When she did, the doctor asked me to bring her some broth. Fortunately I had some saved from the chicken and dumplings from when Jane had come to call, and I brought it up on a tray and placed it on the table next to the bed. The doctor was checking her pulse and he murmured a quiet "Thank you." Victoria said nothing and didn't even look in my direction.

I stood and watched as the doctor coaxed Victoria into drinking a few spoonfuls of broth, knowing that it was something I should be doing. I hesitatingly stepped closer and quietly took the bowl out of the doctor's hands. He smiled up at me gratefully, his eyes bleary, and he went to stand to look out the window, rubbing his eyes with his hands.

I turned back to Victoria, who was already glaring at me with unconcealed hatred, and I jumped a little. My hand shook and the spoon clanked against the bowl as I lifted it out to offer it to her. I was angry with myself for being terrified of this woman who couldn't even lift her hand to feed herself. But the fear I had of her had very little to do with the physical harm she could inflict upon me. She was awake and conscious, and the control she usually had over me was now mingled with hatred for my betrayal, and I felt it keenly. She had a piercing way of looking at me that made me feel guilty for keeping my things from her, though I knew it was a perfectly acceptable and necessary thing for me to do. Still, it made my stomach hurt and my heart fill with dread. I tried to push the feeling away, but habit, mingled with my exhaustion and her relentless glare, made it impossible.

I held the shaking spoon up to her lips, the broth spilling a little onto her blankets. After holding my gaze for a moment, she looked away to stare at the opposite wall. I knew how much she hated to accept my help and so I wasn't surprised when she refused it. It reminded me that everything was to be done on her terms. If she had ordered me to feed her, I would have been expected to do so. But since I was offering her help in her time of need, she would not accept it. She had to have the power and control, even if it meant starving to death. She did not accept; she demanded. She was not to be cared for; she was to be succumbed to.

I gasped in surprise when the doctor placed a gentle hand on my shoulder. I don't know if he saw the exchange between Victoria and me, but he quietly suggested I take the soup back to the kitchen and I was all too happy to obey.

I quickly left the room and heard the quiet snoring of my stepsisters echoing through the hall. As I made my way to the kitchen, I noticed all the things that were being left undone. Doing all the cooking for the family and cleaning the entire house, feeding the animals, and tending the garden usually took up all of my time. But now that I had to do all of those things—having had no sleep and caring for a seriously ill woman—I was feeling the strain.

I stood in the kitchen, the tray still in my hands, wondering where to begin, when the sound of my name suddenly broke the silence. The glass bowl clattered loudly against the tray as I spun around to see the doctor looking at me with eyes full of pity. I put the tray down on the table before it could fall from my trembling hands.

"My dear, how are you?" He spoke so gently it made me want to cry.

Whenever I saw the doctor, I remembered those last days of Father's life and how kind he had been to me as I struggled with my father's looming death. I opened my mouth to say I was fine, but instead my face crumpled and I buried my face in my hands. Suddenly his gentle arms were around me, and I cried onto his shoulder. He tenderly patted my back and spoke soothingly.

"There, there. You have such a heavy burden to bear. I'm so sorry. I knew things were not the same here, but I just didn't know how bad they had become." He paused. "I'm so sorry," he said again. He didn't seem uncomfortable at all to have me sobbing on him, even if it was completely out of character for me. He was probably used to it in his line of work. "Ella, dear, what can I do to help you? Is there anyone you know who could help?" He pulled back so he could look at me and got a twinkle in his eye. "A prince, perhaps?"

He was obviously referring to the ball and the very slim possibility of my marrying a prince and perhaps someday not having to worry about any of this anymore. But at the moment, my needs could not be met by a prince.

"Not unless he knows how to milk a cow." I laughed softly through my tears.

"Maybe he has had lessons. You never know," he said, grinning back. I laughed at what I assumed was a joke, and the doctor laughed with me.

He patted my arm, and it felt so grandfatherly that I wanted to hug him again, but I restrained myself. He smiled wearily and said, "Don't you worry, my dear. Everything will work out in the end."

And though I didn't know exactly what "the end" meant, I was so grateful to the doctor for staying the whole night and sharing my burden. I clung to his hope that things would somehow work out. Returning a weary smile of my own, I whispered, "Thank you."

Chapter 12

After the doctor left, I went to check on Victoria. She was sitting up in her bed, as if waiting for me to come back.

"Where are the gown and slippers?" she asked calmly. I stood silently, refusing to answer, though my heart raced. She glanced over to her nightstand where she kept her stick, and her fingers twitched toward it. And then, as if she was too exhausted to care, she slowly lowered her head to her pillow and closed her eyes with a weary sigh. I stood stunned for a moment and then tiptoed out of the room, grateful that it had been unusually easy to escape punishment. I continued with my normal routine, while also feeding, washing, and caring for Victoria. That night, I slept on the chair next to her bed, my head flopping forward every few minutes, waking me up all night.

On Tuesday morning we had the same conversation about the gown and slippers—Victoria asking me where they were and me refusing to tell. Only this time, she whipped my hands pitifully, almost for tradition's sake. It appeared that she was out of ideas and was feeling defeated. When she was done with her pathetic whipping, I hurried out to tend to the garden and the animals.

I returned to the house and ironed the dry laundry. Fatigue seemed to weigh down my arms and my eyelids as I trudged up the stairs to put my stepsisters' clothes away. I was about to enter but stopped when I saw that Mabel and Cecelia weren't in their rooms. They were in mine—my old room I used to sleep in before Father had died. I crossed the hall and glanced inside the open doorway. There wasn't much left in there—a nightstand and an empty wardrobe—but everything had been overturned and thoroughly destroyed.

They were searching.

I listened in the hall as they ruined furniture and looked in corners and behind curtains.

"Why would we go to Roger's party if we're going to marry the prince?" Cecelia asked.

I could almost hear Mabel roll her eyes. "How are *we* going to marry the prince? He will only be able to marry one of us." And by "us" she clearly meant herself. "So the other will have to marry the next best thing." And by "best" she obviously meant richest. "Now, come on. We must find Ella's things or no one will marry us."

As conniving and foolish as they were, I couldn't help laughing quietly to myself as I continued with my chores, while also feeling relieved that they were as far away from finding my things as they could be. Soon after, they left to attend Roger Wallace's hastily planned welcome home party—a party that was surely moved up about a month so it could be held before the ball to remind all the young ladies what a catch Roger Wallace thought he was.

***

MY WHIPPING THE NEXT MORNING HAD A LITTLE MORE potency behind it. Either Victoria was getting angrier with me, or she was getting stronger. I knew Victoria was trying to break me, to force me into succumbing to her, but surprisingly, every whip of my hands only strengthened my resolve to keep my precious things hidden from her. After our daily exchange, I went about my routine of keeping the house in order and Victoria alive.

But by late morning, I was utterly exhausted. My hands bled constantly and made every task almost unbearable. I was still determined, but that didn't mean there wasn't pain. I had so much to do, but I would find myself wandering around the house, not being able to think clearly enough to figure out what I should be doing. I would stand motionless, staring out of a window, when I would suddenly realize that I was supposed to be washing it. I would walk into a room and have to stand there for five minutes before I remembered what I was supposed to be doing, only to realize I was in the wrong room. The vegetables needed to be harvested. The laundry was piling up. I had cream to separate and butter to churn and corn to grind and a dying woman to keep alive.

I decided it was time to recruit some help. I found some in the form of two very spoiled, very unwilling, very angry stepsisters. I ignored their offended looks at being ordered around by someone they saw as their servant, and soon started enjoying myself immensely.

"Please get fresh water for your mother's basin, Mabel," I said for the second time. Mabel was sitting on a chair in the corner of Victoria's room, her arms folded across her chest. She gaped at me as if I had just asked her to part the Red Sea. I would have thought her expression was comical if I wasn't completely fatigued and at the end of my patience. "I have been whipped enough times to know exactly how to use that thing," I added evenly, looking toward the drawer that held Victoria's whipping stick.

Mabel jumped out of bed and ran past me without a word.

I could not hide my smile as I watched her fly down the stairs. Of course, I never would have whipped her, but the threat was effective, though I did feel a twinge of guilt for threatening at all. I had already asked Cecelia to gather the dirty laundry from off the floors in their bedrooms. Cecelia hadn't put up much of a fight, except to stammer and then to cry. I could hear her whimpering in the next room as she picked up the clothes. The sound was as beautiful as the birds chirping outside.

It's true I was worn out and out of patience, but in just a few short days, I had also grown bold and confident, knowing that I could take some initiative and Victoria could do nothing about it. I found a stronger voice than I had ever had and I was not afraid to use it.

Mabel returned with the water and stood in the doorway. It was nice to have help, but it was also frustrating. I could do everything in half the time my stepsisters did, but while they were unwillingly doing the things I asked them to do, I could tend to other things. While I waited for the new water, I washed the windows in Victoria's room, dusted the table that the basin sat on, changed and fluffed Victoria's pillows, and was smoothing her blankets by the time Mabel returned.

"Thank you," I whispered. "Will you please pour it into the basin?" They had to be told everything! Mabel did as she was asked, resentment in each arduous, angry movement, and she dashed out of the room before I could ask her to do anything else.

Victoria moaned a little and I leaned in closer so I could hear if she said anything. After a few moments of silence, I decided she must be hurting even in her sleep. I felt completely helpless, not knowing how to help her or make the pain go away. I changed the cloth on her forehead, and she grimaced a little. I waited until she was still again and quietly walked out of her dark and gloomy room. I still had to feed Mary and milk Lucy, who was certainly going to be annoyed at having to wait so long that morning.

As soon as I entered the hall, I was shocked to see that the sun was shining brightly through the east windows. Knowing that Lucy would soon be mooing loudly to be milked, I started running. I couldn't believe I hadn't heard her yet. I bolted down the stairs and saw Cecelia sulking in a corner at the bottom of the stairs.

"Please go and sit with your mother," I said.

Cecelia crossed her arms, planted her feet on the stone floor, and scowled back at me. I paused and gave her one firm look, and she stomped her way up the stairs. The sound made me smile. I made sure she actually went in to sit with her mother and not just hide out in her own room. Once Cecelia was safely in Victoria's room, I ran to the kitchen to head out the back door. But as I ran around the corner into the kitchen, I came to an abrupt stop.

"Nicely handled," Will said. He was standing by the fire, warming his hands. It took me a moment to realize it wasn't me who had started the fire.

"What are you doing here? And *when* did you get here?" I cried. I felt my face break into a wide smile, touched with bewilderment and relief.

"The doctor dropped by and asked if I'd help out." He shrugged, as if saving my life and my sanity was a minor thing. "That cow is the most spoiled cow in the world," he said. "I've never seen a cleaner stall."

"Well, there's just the one cow." It was my turn to shrug like it was an inconsequential thing, but I smiled. It felt nice to be complimented on my hard work, and even nicer to have someone help me who I didn't have to beg and threaten.

"And that pampered chicken! She doesn't like me much, that's for sure." He laughed, remembering what must have been terrible treatment. "I fixed the gate to the pasture so it can close all the way now, and I repaired that hole in the roof of the stable. I know there aren't any horses in there now, but it might as well be ready for when there are." He said it with such confidence that I couldn't help feeling hopeful that one day there might be horses in the stable again. "Oh, and you shouldn't have to worry about restocking the wood pile any time soon, and I replaced the bottom step of the front porch so I don't have to worry about you twisting your ankle every time you use it."

I stood there with my mouth hanging open. I was over-whelmed with gratitude.

"Will, I don't know how to thank—"

"No, don't thank me, Ella. I wouldn't have even told you except I didn't want you to worry about them anymore." He sighed and lowered his head. "I feel terrible. I had no idea how sick Victoria was. I'm so sorry. I can't imagine what your week has been like." He looked at me when he noticed my stunned silence. "How are you?"

"Wonderful, now!" I cried. "I can't thank you enough for coming. I never could have done all those things! And poor Lucy would not have liked me very much this morning." I laughed and then cringed, remembering the time I had waited too long to milk Lucy last spring. I had been too sick to get out of bed so early and Lucy had kicked me in the stomach as soon as I got close to her. I had not been late since.

"I'm happy to help. It's been busy at the palace this week, but I'm glad to see you've enlisted some help in the mean-time." He glanced upward toward the upstairs bedrooms and winked.

"They're not too thrilled about it," I said, laughing quietly, looking over my shoulder to make sure no one could hear us.

"You have done some pretty amazing things in your life,

but getting those spoiled rotten, good-for-nothing girls off their lazy behinds tops them all!" Will cried, apparently not too concerned about who heard him.

"They put up quite a fight at first, but I must be pretty convincing when I threaten because they have been quite compliant." I became serious and turned my gaze to the hypnotic flames of the fire. "I just couldn't do it all myself. I couldn't keep up with all of the chores and take care of their sick mother." I paused and glanced quickly over my shoulder once more. "I always knew they were heartless and cruel, but to see their lack of concern over Victoria's obviously deteriorating health is beyond my comprehension."

"Of course it is," Will said matter-of-factly as he put some more wood on the fire. "You don't know how to not care for people, so when you see that level of callousness, you can't understand it." He brushed off his hands and stood up, placing a hand on the mantle and staring at the flames. "You're so kind, Ella, that you can't comprehend unkindness."

I was surprised by this insight he had, as if he had already noticed this about me and it was just blatantly obvious. I remembered seeing Father that way and thinking that his incomprehension of coldness and cruelty must be the reason he married Victoria. He was all heart, and if he had seen any hints of her heartlessness, he wouldn't have believed it. I could at least see it, but it didn't make it any easier to grasp or endure.

I blinked and looked away from the heat that was burning my eyes. "You're kind too, Will. How can you stand it?"

"Because I've been out in the world more than you have. Maybe not very much more, but I've seen people do terrible things and say terrible things." He looked down at me. "But I've never seen or heard anyone more terrible than Victoria. She is vicious. The way she treats you puts every other mean person I have ever met to shame. And yet, you tolerate it day after day. I understand why you do it. I know you promised to take care of them. But that doesn't make it any easier for me to believe . . ." He turned back to face the fire and whispered, ". . . or bear."

I didn't know what to say. Will had rarely brought up the subject since I had told him about my promise years before and I was surprised by how troubled he was by it. I never thought about it anymore. It was pointless. I had already chosen.

Will changed the subject after a thoughtful silence. "Did you know I'm going be at the ball?" He smiled up at me, all hints of his previous melancholy erased.

"Really? Oh, I just knew you had a secret desire to live a life of luxury. You just couldn't stand to stay away," I joked.

"No, thank you. No life of snobby extravagance for me. The prince has asked all the servants to help on the night of the ball. The groomsmen will tend to all the horses while the guests arrive, and then we'll be *allowed*"—he rolled his eyes—"to enter the palace and serve all the fancy people." Will grimaced. "I have to walk around with a glass tray and serve the guests drinks and food. They've been training us unrefined stable workers how to properly balance a tray on our hands. It's beyond insulting. I have to wear a ridiculous suit and everything."

"Ridiculous? Impossible. You'll look so handsome!"

Will smiled. "Does that mean you'll be there to see me looking so handsome?"

I thought of my dress and gown hidden away under the floorboards in my tower. How would I possibly wear them without Victoria knowing? But if I didn't wear them now, when would I ever get to? A part of me desperately wanted to go, but another part of me couldn't even imagine it.

"You really should come. With me looking so handsome and everything, who knows what could happen? There will be an alarming number of single ladies there, you know." He chuckled softly to himself and held his hands up to the fire to warm them again.

I laughed with him, soaking in the warmth of the fire. "I feel like I'm always saying this to you, but thank you. You're the kindest friend I've ever had . . . the kindest friend anyone has ever had."

Will looked down at me, a soft expression in his eyes. He started to smile when a shadow crossed over his face. Then swiftly, for the first time ever, he wrapped his arms around me and held me close to him. He held me tightly. It was as if he were trying to show me I wasn't alone but couldn't say it with words. I felt a spark of something inside me. It felt like an emotion a living person might feel, not just someone who was merely surviving.

This was different than when the doctor had held me. It was different but the same. I felt comforted and strengthened, but I wasn't sure how I felt about the fluttering in my stomach and the flush in my cheek. I must be standing too close to the fire.

I pulled away and looked out the window, then at the fire, and then I looked down, obviously and awkwardly avoiding Will's eyes. I felt embarrassed and confused by my sudden shyness so I tried to think of something to say. I could feel Will's eyes on me, burning with unusual intensity, and he seemed to sense what I was going to say.

"I better get back to work," we both said.

"Then it must be true," he said with a smile.

Chapter 13

WHEN I RETURNED TO FEED VICTORIA HER MIDDAY MEAL, I came to an abrupt stop outside the door. Mabel and Cecelia were in Victoria's room, which was astonishing, but what they were saying was even more so.

"The dress maker won't let us take out any more credit," Mabel was whining. "We begged and begged and he refused! If only we had bought ball gowns when we were in town instead of afternoon dresses, then we wouldn't be in this mess!"

"It was your idea!" Cecelia shouted.

Victoria sighed angrily. "Well, then, you *must* find the gown and slippers. I can't do everything around here!" she said hoarsely. "Tear the house apart!"

I knew they were searching for my things, but to hear the level of desperation in their voices and the way they spoke about things that were not theirs—and would never be theirs—filled me with anger that made me bold. Taking a deep breath to steady myself, I entered the room and casually walked to the side of Victoria's bed.

"Would you like your broth now?" I asked as if there was nothing strange about their conversation.

Mabel and Cecelia exchanged guilty looks and quickly left the room. I fed Victoria her broth as she glared at me.

***

ON THURSDAY MORNING, I WAS ASLEEP ON THE CHAIR NEXT to Victoria's bed, my head resting on my folded arms on the mattress. I never would have felt comfortable being so close to her, letting my weary head share her bed. But it had become necessary for me to remain close to her should she need anything through the night—a cool cloth, water, a basin, a blanket.

I felt her looking at me and I raised my eyes to meet her emotionless face, which was lit dimly by what little light streamed in from her open door.

"Eggs" was all she said.

I was only in my nightgown, but I ran out to the henhouse and gathered two eggs and quickly threw Mary some kernels while I was out there. I was grateful that Mary had made up for Martha's absence, at least for that day. I fried up the eggs and brought them to Victoria, who ate one of them and pushed the plate away.

Before she fell back to sleep, she again asked me where the gown and slippers were, I refused to answer, and she whipped my hands as she had all week. I left the room to get dressed and woke Mabel and Cecelia to look after their mother while I was away. They started to whine in their already whiny voices, but they didn't refuse.

I dressed quickly, started a fire in the kitchen fireplace, and noticed the dust accumulating on the floors and the sewing that needed to be done. I wondered if I'd ever get back on top of things. I fixed a quick breakfast for Mabel and Cecelia and milked Lucy and washed and hung the laundry. I stripped the bed linens and washed and hung them out with the rest of the laundry. Victoria's bed sheets were in desperate need of changing, but I was terrified of moving her.

I went out to the garden and harvested a few potatoes, carrots, and onions, and some more corn. I smiled as I remembered the poem Mrs. Gibb, our last remaining cook, had taught me. She told me to be generous in planting my seeds, saying, "One for the woodchuck, one for the crow, one for the slug, and one to grow." She taught me to plant when the oak leaves were the size of a squirrel's ear, or when the hickory buds were as big as a crow's bill. She had been right and I was forever grateful to her for teaching me to live off of our land, instead of needing to buy everything we ate with money we didn't have.

Mrs. Gibb had stayed at Ashfield long after all the other servants had left. When I was twelve I had asked her how she stayed even though she was receiving no wages.

"The Lord provides for me, my darling, so I can help provide for you," she said.

Mrs. Gibb died at Ashfield, serving our family until her last breath. I was thirteen. I still thought of her strong, yet withered hands every time I kneaded bread. I would always remember the way she smacked her wrinkled lips and smiled in satisfaction when she sampled the soup before it was to be served. I admired her absolute refusal to give up on a pan that had been scorched and watched her scrub the blackness out by the light of the fire until it looked brand new. It reminded me of how she would never give up on me—a little girl who was not born to work in the kitchen or tend the garden—but she taught and trained me tirelessly and it was not until I was as prepared as I could be that she was finally able to rest.

Today, as I worked, I couldn't help thinking about the ball. One of my greatest fears about the ball was that it would be life changing. If I said that out loud to anyone who knew anything about my life, they would think I had lost my mind. But the thought wasn't irrational to me. My life was not perfect, but it was mine, and I worried that going to the ball would make me less satisfied with this life. Could I really come home and work like a peasant after spending an evening feeling like a princess?

But then a thought entered my mind—a forbidden thought. What if I did go to the ball and the prince did notice me? What if he did want to marry me? Could I leave my home? Who would take care of it? Who would take care of Victoria, Cecelia, and Mabel? I was confused by how torn I felt. Then I chuckled to myself. I was sure I wouldn't have to worry about any of that. If I were to go, it would simply be to experience a night of beauty and freedom, not to win over a prince.

As soon as I truly realized that I didn't have to fight for anything or prove anything—that I could just go and enjoy myself—I could see how foolish I'd been. I could go to the ball. I could wear my beautiful things. I could come home and live the life I always had, keeping the memory of the ball with me. Of course I would go to the ball. The only thing stopping me was myself.

Happiness began to bubble up inside of me that felt like it had been there all week, just waiting for me to make this decision. The ball was tomorrow! I thought about how relieved I was that I didn't have to worry about miraculously coming up with the money to buy a new gown to wear; or, more likely, to not be able to buy one at all and having to stay home for that reason. I smiled to myself, knowing that I have had a beautiful gown waiting for me for as long as I could remember.

Before I really knew what I was doing, I dropped my basket of vegetables and ran toward the house. I hadn't really looked at my gown and slippers since the day the ball was announced and only briefly as I hurriedly hid them away from Victoria on Sunday, and I was excited to look at them in this new light—this new light of feeling worthy enough to go, to actually wear them. I ran through the kitchen and up the stairs. When I reached Victoria's room, I listened for any sound. All was quiet in there, so I assumed she was sleeping. And even though I had asked them to look after Victoria, Mabel and Cecelia were arguing in Mabel's room about what they were going to wear to the ball and what the other one could or could not borrow. I could hear the desperation in every word.

"The ball is tomorrow and I don't even have a gown and we haven't been able to find Ella's!" Mabel whined.

"Jane said you could wear her pink gown and pearls!" Cecelia cried back.

"But I want a *new* dress!" Mabel sounded close to tears. "And I'm the oldest. If the prince marries anyone, it should be me. How is he going to notice me in some old dress?"

"You? Why would the prince want to marry you? I . . ."

I hurried past the door before they could hear me. I would only be gone for a few minutes and they were obviously busy. I had never looked at my things when they were home, but they had never been up to my tower that I knew of, and they didn't know—or care—where I was anyway.

I flung open my door at the top of the stairs and warily looked behind me. When I was sure everyone was still downstairs, I closed the door and crouched down on the floor. I quickly and silently lifted the floorboards to look once more at my beautiful gown and exquisite slippers.

Unlike the last time I looked at my last and most valued possessions, I didn't feel an overwhelming sense of unworthiness. I looked at the mud under my fingernails, the calluses on my palms, and the lines from my most recent whipping and I realized they were beautiful hands. These hands worked and sacrificed. They weren't idle or frail. They were strong and they were beautiful in a way no one else could understand, in a way even I didn't understand, but was beginning to appreciate. I no longer felt unworthy of my dress and shoes. I now saw that they were worthy of me.

I felt an overpowering happiness fill my soul. My hands

ached to touch my dress and put on my shoes. I was ready to wear them and be able to see myself on the outside the way I now felt on the inside. I was afraid to lose this elating feeling of self-worth and confidence, but I would have to find a way to keep it without the help of pretty clothes, knowing that now was not the time to put them on. I clung to the feeling and told myself that I must not forget the clarity I felt at this moment.

Cold panic raced through my veins at the alarming sound of frantic footsteps pounding on the creaky stairs up to my tower. I hastily covered my dress with its protective paper. I quickly pushed two of the floorboards into place, but as I was sliding the last one in, the door flew open. I didn't turn around to see who it was. I knelt on the ground for half a second, still as stone, deciding if I should secure the board, or turn around and risk my gown being seen. With trembling hands I secured the last board into place. I even grabbed a corner of my apron and pretended to scrub something off the floor, praying that I looked nonchalant.

I turned calmly around to see Cecelia standing in the doorway, purple and panting. I swiftly rose to my feet, ran over to her, and grabbed the tops of her arms. I instantly felt guilty for sneaking past Victoria's silent room without checking on her. Victoria must be dead.

"Mother's awake and I don't know what to do!" Cecelia gasped, and she shook my hands off her.

I amazed myself by not rolling my eyes and instead told her it would be fine. She scrutinized my small room and then nodded, gulping in more air. She followed me down the stairs, hiccupping all the way. As we descended, I forced myself to be calm. Cecelia couldn't have seen anything, I kept telling myself. Surely she hadn't come up to my tower to see if the dress and slippers were up there. I refused to think the worst because . . . it was unthinkable. When we reached Victoria's door, I wasn't surprised when Cecelia returned to her room as quickly as she could before I could ask her to do something.

I knocked softly on the door. There was no answer, but I decided I better check on her. She was too ill to be left alone for long and Cecelia had said she was awake. I tried to quietly open the door, and winced as it creaked the whole way.

"Are you awake, Stepmother?" I whispered. I truly did want to know if Victoria was actually awake, but I certainly didn't want to be the one to wake her.

"Not for long," said Victoria's weak voice.

I crossed the room to stand at the foot of her bed. Victoria was sitting up slightly, propped up against her pillows.

"You look better," I observed. "Are you hungry?"

An uncomfortable silence followed, and I shifted my weight on my bare feet. The fear that had dissipated during the last few days when Victoria had been so ill was returning. I almost felt ashamed of the courage and confidence I had felt at being free to run the house for the first time. Almost.

"How could I be better with you standing there? How could I be better with you anywhere near me?" Victoria's thin lips were tense and her eyes flashed with hatred. Her arms trembled visibly as she pushed herself up off the pillows so she could be more upright. "I hate that you have deceived me and that my daughters have nothing to wear to the ball. I hate that I am going to die in this wretched house that I have hated every single day for the past ten years. I hate that it is you who has kept me alive. And I *hate* that I had to marry that fool who left me here with you."

At the mention of my father and the way Victoria spoke about him, my breath whooshed out of my lungs. I clenched my teeth so hard if felt like they would shatter, and my hands balled into fists, my fingernails digging into the tender skin on my palms.

"How dare you!" I hissed through my teeth.

While there were times that I had chosen to stay silent rather than speak to Victoria, I had never spoken to her in anything less than the most respectful tone. She was still trembling with rage from her own outburst, but without looking away from me, she reached over to the table next to her bed and opened the drawer that I knew well.

"Come here, child." The term was not one of endearment, but a reminder of my subservience—a reminder that Victoria was the master here. I forced my feet to move toward her. To my astonishment, Victoria slowly slid her emaciated legs out from under her quilts and placed her skeletal feet on the floor. She panted as she laboriously raised herself to her full height, a full five inches above mine.

"Hold out your hands," she said coldly.

I lifted both my trembling hands and held my palms out. Victoria raised her frail arm, a vindictive smile across her dry, cracked lips. The stick came down with an ominous whirr through the air and as it came in contact with my sore, work-roughened hands, I caught it.

"No!" I said, my voice ringing with authority that Victoria had never heard. I snatched the stick out of Victoria's hand, snapped it in two, and then threw it across the floor. "You will never strike me again."

Victoria stood motionless for a moment, her mouth hanging open, her eyes full of fury. Then she collapsed on her bed from exhaustion and utter amazement. I turned to leave the room, but Victoria's alarmingly cool and powerful voice stopped me.

"I hope you weren't planning on going to the ball tomorrow tonight. You're not going anywhere after that outrageous display," she said calmly from her bed.

My rage still surged within me, giving me courage. "How are you going to stop me?"

"Because I am going to be there and I will see to it that you are thrown out if you so much as peek inside the gates." And with a satisfied chuckle, she placed her head back on her pillows.

I turned my back on her, not waiting to be dismissed. I closed the door, muting Victoria's soft laughter.

***

I STOOD IN THE HALL FOR A LONG TIME, CLUTCHING ONTO the railing that overlooked the living room—seeing nothing, feeling nothing. My hopes were dashed to pieces, but the pieces hadn't hit the ground yet so I couldn't grasp the impact.

As soon as Victoria spoke the words forbidding me from going to the ball, I knew she never had any intention of letting me go. She had waited for the hope to build so she could crush it at just the right moment.

I was dimly aware of the sunlight's weakening rays moving across the faded walls. A part of me knew that I should go get my vegetables that I had left in the garden. I knew I should be bringing Lucy back into the barn. I had a million other things I should be doing, but I couldn't make myself do them. I clung to the railing as if it was the only solid thing in my world. A chill crept into the house making my teeth chatter and my body shiver and I knew the fire in the kitchen must have died out.

After what could have been mere minutes or many hours, the front door opened and Mabel and Cecelia sauntered in the house. I didn't even know they had been gone. They were each carrying large boxes and they went straight up to Victoria's room. I didn't care what was in their boxes nor did I turn to watch them enter the room behind me and close the door. I heard their squeals and cackles, but I had no desire to see what all the excitement was about.

After a while, I was assaulted by pink and yellow as Mabel and Cecelia waltzed out of Victoria's room wearing what could only be their new ball gowns. They were so scandalously low in the neckline they looked like they would be wearing them to a brothel, not a ball.

The material was obviously expensive. There were frills and pleats and ruffles any place they could possibly be sewn in. The dresses were completely ridiculous and obnoxious, perfectly matching the personalities of their wearers, I mused without emotion. I ignored their spinning and their giggles that somehow still managed to be whiny.

I didn't know where I was going, but found myself moving in the direction of the door at the end of the hall, the door that led to my tower. As I walked, my steps became quicker and my heart began to race. I didn't know if the enormity of what Victoria had said to me was finally sinking in or if I just desperately needed to be away from the twirling girls. As my pace quickened, I had the awful sensation that I was being chased.

I reached the door at the end of the hall, violently threw it out of my way, and frantically raced up the stairs three at a time, grabbing the rickety banister and hurling myself forward, which resulted in slivers being shoved into my hands as I tripped over my dress and painfully slammed my body against the stairs. I reached my door and hurled it open with a crash. Suddenly I knew why I was there, and my whole body went cold and hot at the same time.

I fell to the ground and grabbed at the floorboards, throwing them out of my way and revealing the empty space underneath. My hands flew to my face and then clutched at my throat. I let out a cry that sounded hauntingly like the last note I had played on my violin in the cellar years ago, a keening that had lingered in the stillness.

Chapter 14

I BARELY JUMPED WHEN I HEARD A GENTLE KNOCKING AT the back kitchen door. My tears had run dry and I had been sitting in a stupor, watching the fire crackle for what seemed like hours. What good had my glimpse of self-worth done me when it was up against Victoria's dominance and my stepsisters' treachery?

I stood with a sigh and went to answer the door. Will stood there, his expression radiating complete happiness as usual, but it fell immediately when he took in whatever emotion was on my face.

"What happened? Is Victoria dead?" His tone sounded more hopeful than upset.

"No," I replied vacantly. I left the door open for him to come in and returned to my chair by the fire.

"I guess I should have known. I don't think you would look so sad if that were the case," he joked lightly, trying to cheer me up.

I had gone back to watching the flames.

"Ella?" His voice had turned soft and imploring.

I shook my head. I couldn't talk about it yet. He knew from experience that it was useless trying to make me talk about what was bothering me. I would bring it up if I wanted to.

Will cleared his throat. "How do you like my suit?" he asked. He was trying to sound cheerful, but I could hear the hesitation in his voice.

Forcing my eyes from the dancing flames, I looked at him and noticed what he was wearing. For a moment, I forgot my sadness and admired how handsome he looked. He was wearing his uniform for the ball—a long, dark-blue suit coat with matching pants. The coat was secured up all the way to his chin with brass buttons that ran all the way down the front. He had shiny black shoes on. He stood tall as I appraised him, though he looked as uncomfortable as he must have felt.

"All right. That's enough ogling." He laughed as he unbuttoned the top button of his collar. "I didn't only come to show off how incredible I look." He winked. "I was wondering if you could sew the sleeve for me. I was going to have one of the palace seamstresses do it, but they had left by the time I noticed it. They must have taken my measurements wrong and I tore the seam of the sleeve. Or maybe my muscles have grown since they measured me." He chuckled, and I couldn't help smiling a little.

I walked across the room to get my sewing kit that sat on top of a pile of clothes that needed mending. When I returned, Will was standing by the fire wearing his white button-up shirt, his suit coat in his hands. As I walked past him, his hand gently grasped my arm.

"You don't have to, Ella. I know you have a lot to do . . ." As he spoke, I took the coat, sat down, and started to sew.

"Yes, and this is the most important. I'm happy to help, Will. It's the least I can do," I murmured.

After a few minutes, the seam was repaired and I handed the coat back to Will.

"Thank you," he said, folding the coat over a chair. "I can't even tell where the tear was. You're amazing, Ella!"

I smiled at him, but then my face crumpled and I buried my face in my hands. Suddenly, Will was kneeling in front of me, his hands on my arms. He pulled my hands away from my face and tenderly wiped the tears from my eyes.

"I'm going to get you away from Victoria somehow, Ella." Underneath the softness in his voice, I heard the now-familiar determination.

My chin quivered. "She told me I can't go to the ball. I had finally decided to go and she took it away from me." I quickly recounted the story for Will. I told him what she had said about my father and how she hated this house. Then, reluctantly, I told him about what happened with Cecelia in my room and how she discovered my secret. I had been careless and vain, and I would never forgive myself. My voice trembled as I told him how my dress and glass slippers had been sold to pay for Mabel and Cecelia's vile, gaudy dresses, just as Victoria had sold Father's violin to pay their debts.

Will listened in horrified silence. "Those two twits stole your dress and shoes? That half-dead wretch is getting up out of her deathbed to keep you from going to the ball? Not if I have anything to say about it." He spoke with such conviction that I felt a tiny glimmer of hope.

As soon as I felt that hope, I unexpectedly had an idea, but I wasn't going to tell Will about it. He would try to stop me or come up with his own idea, and I wouldn't allow it. In the moment I made the decision, I felt completely at peace and my mind was made up.

Will continued to kneel in front of me, and I watched him as he stared into the fire. Will and I had come to depend on each other. We saw each other nearly every day but our relationship had always stayed the same—comfortable, yet reserved; courteous, but careful; friendly, but not intimate—until this week. A change had taken place and I couldn't quite identify where it had come from. Perhaps it was with the announcement of the ball; or Father being gone for ten years; or Victoria's declining health; or maybe it was feeling like he was my only friend now that Jane had been pulled away from me. Will and I had grown closer this week, and I truly looked at him for the first time.

Had there always been gold in his green eyes, or was it just the firelight flickering in them? Did he always look so mature, or was it because his face was brooding at the moment? How long had his shoulders been broad enough to carry his own burdens as well as lighten mine?

His dark hair fell across his forehead carelessly, and I suddenly wanted to brush it back away from his eyes. The fire illuminated his sharp features but also brought a softness to them, creating a contrast between his straight nose and defined cheekbones and his gentle eyes and smooth mouth.

I was beginning to actually feel, and that was dangerous. When I felt, I hurt. And Victoria knew that and used that. I had become a survivor, someone who merely stayed alive, not lived; not felt—at least, not deeply—if I could help it. Had this distance between Will and me been my doing? Did he notice the careful space between us?

He felt my gaze on him and he looked back at me. His eyes were still intense but not angry. I blushed at being caught staring at him and I tried to speak before it became more awkward. I decided to tell him what I had been wondering about. The gap between us had closed enough that I felt I could speak honestly.

"Will, I've been thinking." My voice was soft, but not timid. "Why hasn't anything ever happened between us? I mean, most of the girls my age are married and many have babies. The men your age are off seeking their fortunes or married themselves." My tone lightened as I spoke, not wanting to scare him or make it too serious. I was simply curious. Maybe he had answers I didn't.

His eyes watched me intently. He placed his hands over mine, which were now resting on my lap. I was trying to keep the conversation light, but he was not taking it lightly. He leaned in closer to me.

"I've never had anything to offer you," he said softly. I was surprised that he actually had an answer. I thought he would laugh and say he didn't know either. But I couldn't make sense of his answer. What was he referring to? Worldly goods, a comfortable home . . . love? Was that what he couldn't offer me? Is that why we had always remained respectfully reserved?

His eyes were unrelenting as he searched my face, seeming to look for answers to his own questions, and I couldn't catch my breath. He didn't say anything else and he made no indication that he would. He just looked back at me, holding my hands, saying nothing.

"Why have you never kissed me?" I couldn't believe I asked the question, but at the same time, I had to know and I didn't know when, or if, I'd ever muster the courage to ask him again.

He leaned in even closer, and I watched his eyes flicker to my lips. He raised one hand to touch my cheek, his fingers caressing my skin as lightly as a breeze. He seemed to be debating over something, but he never looked away from my face. There was an intensity in his eyes that was different than when I'd seen him angry or serious or pensive. It made my bones feel like liquid.

I watched countless emotions play across his face and they mesmerized me. At last, his features relaxed and they composed themselves into an expression I recognized but couldn't put a name to.

He dropped his hand from my face, his other hand let go of mine, and he pulled away from me. I was sitting next to the blazing fire but I instantly felt chilled. He grabbed his coat and turned back to me with a solemn expression.

"You were never mine to kiss," he whispered.

He sighed so quietly I could have imagined it, and walked out the door.

As soon as he left, I realized what his expression was. It was resignation—and I saw it every time I looked in the mirror.

Chapter 15

I DIDN'T GO TO SLEEP. I STARED AT THE DOOR FOR A LONG time after Will left, trying to make sense of what he had said and the expression on his face as he left. I worried that I had scared him, despite my best intentions, and wondered if I should have kept quiet, while also being grateful that I hadn't. I hoped I hadn't ruined our relationship. I could barely believe the things I had said now that I was sitting alone in the empty kitchen and my face flushed from the memory.

I contemplated our conversation until my thoughts were a chaotic, tired mess, and I forced them to the back of my mind. I waited until any footsteps upstairs were silent and the house became still. I wrapped my shawl around me and ducked out into the cool night.

I took the shortcut into town through the woods. It was the first time in my life that I could remember being afraid of the forest and what could be lurking behind any tree in the darkness. Every twig that snapped made my heart leap out of my chest. Once an owl hooted and I screamed out loud in terror. My hands trembled, and not from the cold, as they held my thin shawl tight around me. I had left my hair down, hoping it would provide just a little more warmth as it swirled around me and hung heavily down my back.

Victoria had forbidden me from going to the ball. A day or two before, I would have smiled in secret after hearing her threat knowing that I wasn't planning on going anyway and that her punishment would have been futile. I never would have admitted as much to her or she would have found some other way to punish me. But once I had decided that I would go, that I was worthy to go, and that I was not going to miss this extraordinary experience, nothing was going to stop me. There were a few hours after Victoria forbade me to go where I felt like all hope was lost and I was going to have to stay home, but Will's resolve was contagious and I knew I needed to take my fate into my own hands.

Sweating and freezing, I burst through the trees and into the center of town. The shops were all closed and there wasn't a single lantern lit, but I knew exactly where the shop I needed was, and if I had to wake the shopkeeper, so be it. We were both going to benefit from this, and I would not take no for an answer.

I came to the shop and knocked softly on the door. No answer. I knocked louder still. No answer. Finally, I balled my hand into a fist and pounded with all my strength and the sound echoed through the eerie silence. The shopkeeper lived in the back room and I saw a dim glow as a candle was lit and then I watched as its faint light illuminated the path of the woman holding it. Finally, the door creaked open and I gasped in fright at the weakly lit face glaring back at me through sleepy eyes.

The old woman scowled. Then, as recognition dawned on her face, a wrinkly smile lit her features, transforming her into a different person. I smiled back, relieved to see that she wasn't too angry with me.

"Miss Blakeley, to what do I owe this pleasure?" she asked cordially as she opened her door, inviting me in. Though her demeanor was kind, I could see her study me shrewdly. I knew she remembered the last time we had spoken.

"I want to sell my hair," I stated without emotion.

"Miss Blakeley, I told you years ago, you shouldn't be worrying your pretty little head about money," she chided as she let me in and closed the door behind me. I was instantly enveloped in the warmth and safety of her little shop. My eyes swept unwillingly over the room, looking at the dozens of wigs that lined the walls. I gulped and returned to look at the woman.

"I need to sell my hair. Now."

"Why, my child?" There was definite concern in her eyes now.

"I need to buy back something that was stolen from me." I kept my head high and willed my chin not to tremble.

Her eyes tightened infinitesimally. "What was stolen from you?"

I couldn't answer. I didn't trust my voice, nor did I want to tell her what it was and have her decide if a gown and shoes were worth the sacrifice I was willing to make for them. My mind was made up, and I wouldn't let her turn me away this time.

She nodded somberly and pursed her wrinkled lips thoughtfully. "Was it a gown and something else in a little blue box?" she asked.

My eyes widened and filled with tears, and I knew she had her answer.

She nodded again in understanding. "Dear, I saw your sisters waltz into town this afternoon. One had a gown folded in her arms and the other was carrying a box. I knew they were up to no good and I watched them. They went in the dress shop across the road, carrying those things, and came out with their own new dresses and the nastiest looks I've ever seen. Before he closed up shop, I went and asked Mr. Sims, the dress shop owner, how much he would want for the items and asked him to save them. I knew you'd be coming tonight. I'll never forget when you came begging me to cut your hair so you could buy back your violin. Never." Her lips quivered and mine did too. That was one of the worst days of my life. I could again feel my powerlessness and her pity and it only strengthened my resolve.

"Will you cut my hair?" I asked quietly.

She looked back at me for a long time and I refused to look away. I was afraid that if I showed any uncertainty, she would turn me back out into the darkness and its accompanying hopelessness. After a moment, she nodded and picked up her scissors from the table behind her. "I'll only take what I need, dear," she said with a wobbly voice. She led me to a chair in the back of the room and I sat down. She gathered a large chunk of my hair and then I heard the sickening grating, severing sound that turned my stomach. I refused to cry as I heard the first thud of heavy hair hit the ground, though I did feel her tears splashing on my head as she leaned over me to reach for the next portion.

I knew she was done as soon as I felt the last bit of weight fall and I had the strangest sensation that I was floating, even though my hands were clenching the seat of the chair. My head felt incredibly light and my neck and back were suddenly chilled. Unable to avoid looking at the mound of golden hair on the floor, I rose deliberately, hugged the woman gratefully after she placed the money in my trembling hand, and ran across the dirt road to bang on yet another door.

When I placed the money in the groggy Mr. Sims's hand, his eyes widened and he gladly retrieved my beloved dress and slippers and placed them in my eager arms. He turned around with an enormous yawn and shuffled back to bed in his night dress and bed cap, and I ran back home through the woods, my arms and heart full once more.

I stumbled back through the kitchen door a couple of hours before dawn. I was too exhausted to climb the stairs up to my tower, so I placed my dress and slippers in the cellar. There was no reason my stepsisters would look for them, believing they were gone forever, and besides that, I was willing to fight for these things that were precious to me. There was a whisper of warmth left in the smoldering cinders and I lay my head on the hearth—and my feet in front of the cellar doors.

Chapter 16

THE KITCHEN WINDOW FACED WEST, SO I WOULDN'T HAVE the sun's bright morning rays to wake me. Fortunately, I didn't even need them. Once I collapsed on the hearth, I had slept deeply, my mind and heart finally at ease. I blinked in the predawn darkness after only a small amount of sleep, completely alert. I stretched and reached up to feel my chopped-off hair, refusing to be sad over it. To me, it was beautiful. I knew that Father would be proud of me. I had sacrificed something that others would see as pretty for something that was priceless.

No, I was not sad in the least.

In fact, I told myself, it would be easier to get things done, without constantly having to keep my long, thick hair out of my way. The challenge would be keeping the lack of it hidden from Victoria. I wrapped my shawl tightly around my head, stuffing what hair I had left inside and even adding some cloth, so the shawl would appear to be heavy with hair. And though I was covered in cinders and soot, I was already dressed, so I started immediately on my morning chores.

Victoria, Mabel, and Cecelia were up earlier than usual that morning. My stepsisters glared at me with unmistakable superiority, though I refused to meet their eyes and give them the satisfaction. Victoria refused to eat in bed, no doubt trying to remind me that no matter how weak she was, she was stronger than me.

As I stood in my corner, Victoria watched me out of the corner of her eye with a satisfied smile on her lips. I must have looked terrible after getting very little rest and sleeping on dirty stones, but I would let her assume that I was upset over not being able to go to the ball and also over losing my most prized possessions. In reality, I was more resolved than ever to go to the ball—even if I had to walk every step of the way.

I spent the whole day preparing Victoria, Mabel, and Cecelia for the ball. I boiled water for their baths and washed them with the rosewater soap. The delicious scent wafted through the house. Then I dressed them in their magnificent, albeit ostentatious and revolting, gowns.

Bathing and dressing Victoria was like bathing and dressing a corpse for burial. I tried to be gentle as I laced up Victoria's stays and I saw that her corset was too big and had to be taken in, as well as her gown. It was a good thing they had started getting ready so early. I poked myself with the sharp needle a dozen times trying to sew as quickly as I could, the whole time knowing that the only reason I was in such a hurry was so that Victoria could be at the ball to make sure I wasn't.

Mabel and Cecelia did look stunning when I was done with them. Their hair was done in intricate braids all around their heads and their skin was radiant from all the scrubbing and buffing. I wasn't even jealous of their hair that fell past their waists as I braided it. They could have all the hair they could grow and all the pretty dresses they could steal. I had my mother and father back in the form of my gown and slippers, and that was enough for me. And though Victoria could barely hold herself up and she could hardly catch her breath, she could at least pass for a living person when I had finished getting her ready.

I tried to play my role of martyr as best I could. I sighed and sniffled every once in a while, and even tried to shed a tear or two. And even though I may have seemed like the victim in the situation, I felt like the heroine. I had actually taken a little bit of my own fate in my own hands, and it was an exhilarating, heady feeling.

Finally, the time arrived for them to leave. They had arranged with their new best friend, Jane, to drive them to the ball. Our nonexistent driver was still too ill, apparently. Jane's footman knocked on the door to announce her arrival and I answered it in my plain gray dress and dingy apron. I was out of breath and my cheeks were flushed from exertion, and though my hair was tucked tightly into my shawl, a few wild hairs had escaped. The more stunning Victoria, Mabel, and Cecelia became, the more haggard I looked. Jane looked out the window of her carriage and when she saw me her face fell in confusion and dismay.

"Girls, listen to me," Victoria said from behind me. I automatically turned around to listen, though I knew she was only talking to her daughters. "Make sure you are noticed tonight. Find the prince as soon as you can and make him fall in love with you." She looked away from them to survey the house with disgust. "Then maybe we can get out of this place."

My stepsisters smirked as if what Victoria had suggested would even remotely be a challenge and they drifted past me out the door, bumping me out of the way. They strolled to the carriage, their flowing skirts held up to their knees to avoid the dust, and then climbed into the carriage door held open by Jane's footman. For all the material their dresses had, it was quite a feat to show that much skin.

I turned away from the door and rolled my eyes in embarrassment and annoyance. I composed my expression when I saw Victoria watching me from behind and I went to stand by the stairs as she scrutinized me. Victoria slowly turned away from me, hobbled toward the open doorway, and waved to the others who were waiting for her, indicating that she was on her way. As she turned back to face me, I saw her phony smile disappear from her lips and watched it be replaced by a wicked sneer.

"I'll be watching. I may have one foot in the coffin, but I can still make your life miserable, child. I don't have to be alive to make you wish you were dead." Victoria turned, a radiant smile appearing on her face as she stepped out into the dusk.

Jane leaned out the open door of the carriage. "I hope you feel better, Ella! I'm sorry!" I caught a glimpse of Mabel and Cecelia, and they were shaking their heads slowly back and forth in mock melancholy.

Apparently, I must be sick, or more interestingly, having some kind of fit of madness. I couldn't determine if Jane was being sincere or not and decided I didn't care as I listened to their giggling over the pounding of the hooves on the dirt road.

Chapter 17

THE MOMENT THE COACH DISAPPEARED AROUND THE BEND in the road, I dashed to the kitchen where I already had hot water waiting for my bath. Tonight, cold water just wouldn't do. Between bathing, dressing, brushing, buttoning, and braiding the other girls, I had been surreptitiously preparing for when I would get myself ready for the ball. I was more willing than ever to risk any punishment Victoria could think up to enjoy this once-in-a-lifetime experience. What could Victoria do to me that would be worse than what I'd already lived through, anyway?

I chose to make that a rhetorical question.

The warm water felt heavenly, but there was no time for a long, luxurious bath. I washed my short hair, scrubbed my body with the delicious rosewater soap, and dried off. I quickly climbed down the ladder into the cellar, too excited to do anything slowly. My trembling fingers reached into the empty crate hidden under the ladder and pulled back the brown cloth.

My clean hands gently lifted my shimmering pale-blue gown, which had become even more precious to me now that I had had to sacrifice to have it. I carefully draped it over my arm and carried it and the blue box back up to the kitchen. I set the box on the table and picked up the gown by the shoulders and held it up to me. I laughed as I remembered how big it had been when Father had held it up to me; how the hem had dangled on the floor and how disappointed I was that I wouldn't be able to wear it right then. I had thought this day would never come. By the light of the fire, I gently hugged it to me, sixteen years of patient anticipation finally bubbling up to the surface.

I draped my gown over a chair. Before I put it on, I would have to figure out what to do with my hair. It was too short to braid and I couldn't go to the ball with unruly hair. My arms ached as I played with it, trying to persuade it to behave.

Across the kitchen, something caught my eye and I smiled with relief. My knitting needles were sitting on top of a pile of socks that needed to be darned and I darted across the room to them. They were suddenly beautiful to me and not just practical. I wound my hair around them. It was just long enough to be twisted into an elegant bun at the nape of my neck. It may not be the fashionable intricate braids the other girls would have, but I was grateful I had enough hair left to look and feel nice.

I sighed giddily as I gingerly placed the gown over my head and smoothed it down over my body. I closed my eyes as I felt the rich fabric fall like water over my skin. It was heavy with yards and yards of material, but the weight felt comforting and warm, instead of bulky and cumbersome.

I looked down to get a better look at the dress, now that it was finally on. The neckline was a wide oval that reached from shoulder to shoulder and had the same line in the back. The bodice was fitted perfectly and the waistline fell at my ribs. There was intricate embroidery work in white thread at the waist that added a touch of elegance and loveliness. The sleeves were snug from the shoulders to the elbow, and then gently flared out all the way to the wrist.

I saved the skirt for last. It flowed like a waterfall in billowing skirts all around me. I desperately wanted to twirl round, but was afraid of having it anywhere near the fire or anything dirty at all. Even in the glow of the firelight it sparkled like glistening snow.

My hands shook as I leaned over the table and removed the lid off the slippers. They lay there in glass perfection and I lifted the first one out of the box. I held it up so I could admire how it glittered in the fire's light. The slipper was clear, but with a faint blue hue, mingled with orange from the flames.

I marveled at the slipper's beauty for a moment and then bent to place it on my foot. I quickly realized that my skirts would never allow me to reach over to even find my foot, much less put on a fragile shoe. I thought about placing it on the floor and trying to step into it, but I was afraid of shattering it in the process and I was nervous to attempt it anywhere near the fire. I imagined I might have better luck if I sat on the stairs and put them on there, so I placed the slipper back in the box with its match and left the soft, orange glow of the fire.

I stepped out of the kitchen in my bare feet and tip-toed through the dining room and into the foyer. The gentle, smooth light of the moon glowed through the windows in the exact hue of my gown. I felt like I was a part of the moonlight, and that it was a part of me, lighting me from within.

I continued to the stairs, took the shoes out of the box, and placed them side by side on the floor. I was just getting ready to sit on the stairs when I heard the horrifying sound of horse hooves and wagon wheels.

A sickening fear gripped me. Victoria had come back to

make sure I was really staying home. There was no way I could change out of the gown before she came inside. I heard footsteps on the gravel and fled to the dining room and hid behind the wall. I gasped and stuck my head around the corner. In my haste I had left my precious slippers sitting on the floor at the bottom of the stairs.

I clenched my fists and bit down on one of them to keep myself from screaming at myself. I had been careless once, and it had cost me Father's violin. I had been careless again and it had cost me my gown and slippers. Now my carelessness would cost me again. I was too angry with myself to cry, stunned silent with dread.

The door slowly creaked open. My heart pounded in my chest and my ears, making it impossible to hear anything else. The fear was blinding.

"Ella," Will's whispered voice echoed through the empty stone room. "Are you here?"

I dared not make a sound. It could have just been my hope that I heard through the pounding in my brain and not his actual voice. He whispered again, a bit louder this time. I breathed a sigh of relief and laughed at myself for being a coward. My heart still pounding, I emerged sheepishly from my hiding place, stood in the doorway, and grinned in embarrassment.

"I'm sorry. I was hiding," I mumbled. "I thought you were Victoria and I'm a coward." I shook my head. What could Victoria have done to me? Fainted?

"N-No," he stammered. "You're an angel."

I was slowly getting over my fear enough to notice that he was standing still as stone, staring at me with his mouth hanging open.

I laughed. I wanted to disregard his statement, but he had described how I felt. "Thank you," I said with feeling. "You look very handsome yourself." He raised a hand to his freshly cut hair and looked down at the ground, a shy smile on his lips. We were both obviously out of our element.

Will seemed to realize something and stepped closer, his mouth falling open again. But there was something else there now besides admiration. It looked something like disbelief.

"Ella, I was planning on taking you to the ball in your old gray dress whether you wanted to or not. Is this your stolen gown? How did you get it back?" He didn't sound accusatory, but I could tell he suspected I had done something drastic.

"Will, I had to do it." He looked at me more closely, bewilderment and even anger in his eyes. Not anger at me, but anger that I had had to do whatever it was to get my own precious things back that had been stolen in the first place. I laughed softly to try to lighten the mood and slowly turned around. I heard his quiet gasp behind me when he noticed I was missing several feet of blonde hair. "It will grow back, Will," I said as I turned back around. "I don't want you to be sad, because I'm not. I had to do something and I have no regrets. Please don't worry."

He tried to smile and then nodded in acceptance and understanding. "I like it," he said.

I laughed lightly, grateful for his calm reaction. "I need help with my shoes. I can't reach my feet." I hurried back to my beloved slippers that I had abandoned.

Will bolted into action. "Allow me," he said. He knelt down and gently cradled a slipper in his strong hand. It looked like he could crush it into a million pieces with no effort. But he held it up carefully and marveled at it as I had. "I don't know much about shoes, except if they fit or if they hurt my feet, but I can't imagine that there's another pair of shoes like these in the world. Where did they come from?"

"All I know is that they were my mother's," I said, my voice catching in my throat.

He slid the slipper on my outstretched foot and I wondered at its weightlessness. I couldn't resist pointing my toe and admiring how it sparkled. I put my foot down ever so carefully, afraid to put any weight on it. But as soon as I did, I found that though the slipper was made of glass, it felt as durable as diamond. I balanced on my foot and held out my other one. Will placed the other slipper on and then I put both feet on the floor.

"Will, do you mind if I do something I've wanted to do ever since I put this dress on?" I said, my voice bubbling with excitement.

"Not at all," Will said, a bright smile lighting his face.

I held out my arms and spun around in a circle. My skirts rippled like gentle waves around me like when the wind blows across the surface of the pond. It sparkled in the moonlight and my glass slippers faintly clinked against the polished stone. I spun around a few times and then stopped myself abruptly when I felt dizzy. My gown swirled around me as if it wasn't ready to stop yet, and clung to me before it cascaded back to the floor. I grabbed on to Will's arm to steady myself.

"That was the most fun I've ever had!" I said breathlessly.

"Me too."

We laughed together for a moment. Will never looked away from me and I started to feel self-conscious and let go of his arm. The memory of his eyes burning into mine the night before in front of the fire flashed into my mind.

"So, am I recognizable without a torn dress and a dirty face?" I asked, trying to catch my breath and not just from my spontaneous spinning.

Will stepped closer to me, the same burning look in his eyes from last night. Every time I tried to lighten the mood, it had the opposite effect on him. I saw that even in the moonlight, he had those flecks of gold in his green eyes, that it had not just been from the flickering fire. And just as he had last night, he lifted one hand to touch my flushed cheek. Even in the dim light, I was sure he could see and definitely feel my blush, and I ducked my head.

"I have always seen you this way," he said softly, his finger gently pulling my chin up so that I would look at him. My heart pounded peculiarly in my chest and it felt like it took on a mind of its own.

That was all Will said, but he looked like he wanted to say more. Finally, I broke the silence. "Then why are you staring at me like that?" He held my face up to his, but I lowered my eyes.

"Because for the first time, you see yourself clearly." Will smiled. "You are beautiful, Ella. Inside and out. Your father and mother would be proud." He grinned and dropped his hand. But when he did, I kept my own head up and smiled back at him.

I had never felt so close to my mother than at that moment. When I was young, everyone around me spoke of Eleanor with a sense of awe. To me, she had always seemed like a creature from another world. An angel. It had been difficult to try to relate to someone who seemed to be more of a heavenly being than a human being. But looking down at my shimmering dress that flawlessly flowed over me and feeling the perfect fit of mother's shoes on my feet, and feeling the unspeakable joy that filled me inside and out, I finally felt like I was truly my mother's daughter.

An Ember in the Ashes

Chapter 18

WILL LED ME OUT THE FRONT DOOR AND INTO THE SOFT light of the full moon. It was unfiltered and pure and it bathed us in its glow. I couldn't remember a more beautiful night. Perhaps it was because I wasn't pulling Lucy in from the pasture or washing dishes inside the house. How many nights like this had I missed or not taken the time to appreciate? It felt like all my senses were finally waking up from a deep sleep, that I had been a part of a dream and hadn't realized I was sleeping.

Once I soaked up as much loveliness as I could, I couldn't help surveying the yard to make sure no one else was there. For all I knew, Victoria had someone watching me. It seemed safe. Will offered me his arm, and I grasped it, suddenly needing more support than I realized. I gasped when I noticed a glistening, ivory-colored carriage parked in the far end of the front drive. A graceful white horse stood waiting. He seemed impatient.

"Will, where did this come from?" I exclaimed.

Will laughed. "I told you I was tending to the horses tonight. Our assignment was to take the carriages and circle them around so that they would be ready to pick up the guests when the ball ended. This carriage's circle was a little wider than the others," he said innocently.

I shook my head in gentle rebuke but couldn't help feeling like a princess as he opened the door and held his gloved hand out to help me in. I hadn't seen him put on his gloves, but it enhanced the loveliness of the evening even more. I sat on the red velvet cushioned seat and my hands traced the plush fabric that lined the walls.

"I don't know what to say, Will. Besides my father, no one has ever done anything this nice for me." Tears threatened to spill over my cheeks, but I took a breath and steadied myself. "I'm overwhelmed."

"You deserve this, Ella. I just wish you could have this every day." Will's voice unexpectedly faltered at the end of his sentence, and I placed my hand on his arm. My thoughts went to the ball and the realization that I actually could have this kind of life every day. Even when I had decided to go to the ball, it wasn't so I could win over a prince. But now, when I felt like a princess, it seemed as if the possibility was within reach.

Will stood outside the carriage with the door still open. "I think we'd better know the plan before we get there," he said, suddenly serious and practical.

I nodded. I couldn't believe I was going to deceive Victoria like this, right under her nose, in the same room. It was terrifying and exhilarating.

"I will drive you up to the front entrance of the palace. A guard will be there to escort you in. I will have to drive the carriage away, but that will be the last time I'll leave you. I won't exactly be right by your side, but I'll always know where you are and where Victoria is. She will be watching for you."

Chills ran down my spine and I began to shiver. I clenched my teeth to try to steady myself.

"The other thing we have to worry about, besides Victoria seeing you, is making sure anyone else who might mention you to her doesn't see you. We also have to make sure you are home before she is. I saw her pull up tonight in Jane's carriage. Victoria looks awful . . . well, more awful than usual. I don't know how long she's going to last." He smiled. "So make the most of the time you have at the ball."

I nodded again. I was glad Will was taking this seriously. It made me feel less pathetic, hiding from an old and weak woman. We both knew the power Victoria had, but it seemed frivolous and foolish at the same time—taking the risk to go to a silly ball when Victoria could make my life miserable after.

Will lifted his hand to close the door but paused. "One last thing." He dropped his hand from the door and reached out for mine that was still resting on his other arm.

"May I?" He pulled my hand closer to him, bowed over it, and kissed it.

***

MY FRANTICALLY POUNDING HEART FELT LIKE IT WOULD break my ribs. The more I tried to persuade it to calm down, the more determined it was to disobey me and it only beat harder. A part of me could understand its defiance. It didn't want to be contained or controlled. It wanted to beat . . . to live . . . not just keep me from dying.

The carriage drove for miles along the familiar winding road that ran along the edge of the forest and through the main part of town. I caught a glimpse of the wigmaker's shop and couldn't believe that I had been there just the night before, taking my fate in my own hands. We continued on, leaving the shops and buildings behind us, and drove up the hill toward the palace. We reached the massive, ornate iron gates, and two guards with swords hanging from their belts opened them to let us in. Once we were past the gates, the guards closed them behind us with a metallic clang that felt ominously out of place in this beautiful dream.

Ella

We pulled up to the wide, curving front drive of the palace and the carriage came to a stop. Will appeared at the door and opened it. He showed no sign that we knew each other, much less were friends. The only contact we had was when he stiffly held out his hand to help me down. I realized Will probably didn't want anyone to know he had left. Suddenly, I felt terribly guilty, knowing that he was taking so many risks to help me.

When my glass slippers were firmly on the ground, I looked up at the enormous pale gray palace. It glowed silver in the moonlight, and a soft yellow light blazed from within. A small but perfectly manicured garden separated the drive from the front steps and framed the walkway that led up to the palace doors, which were flung wide open. I had spent my whole life looking at this palace but had never fully appreciated its majesty. It was a part of another world. A world I was about to enter, if only for a night.

The sound of the carriage driving away behind me was a poignant indication that I was now alone. Utterly alone. I felt bold and frightened at the same time. I tried to swallow to moisten my suddenly parched throat and walked forward. Almost immediately, a guard was at my side, offering me his arm. I placed my hand on top of his and he led me forward. I smiled my thanks, but he kept his eyes straight ahead the whole time and led me up to the warm light that emanated from the enormous open doors. We ascended the grand staircase, and when we reached the doors, he gently dropped his arm, indicating to me that this is where I continued in alone.

I walked as slowly as possible, knowing that Will would need a few minutes before he returned. There was no sign of anyone in the cavernous foyer, except for the guards spaced evenly apart. I could hear the sound of music and the low hum of hundreds of voices coming from the direction of the line of guards, so I followed it.

As I entered the palace, I admired the gleaming floor and wondered how long it had taken to polish every perfectly cut stone square. I marveled at the countless candles lit in hundreds of perfectly polished candelabras and wondered who had placed and lit each one and who would snuff them out at the end of the night. I gaped at the vaulted ceiling and wondered how they kept it free of cobwebs.

I thought of all the dishes and trays that would be used and who would clean them and who had cooked the food and how long had it taken. I couldn't resist running my fingers over the smooth, dark wood of the decorative tables that were as smooth as glass. Who would clean up when tonight's festivities were over? I smiled, a little guiltily, as I realized that tonight it would not be me.

I reached the gigantic doors that practically vibrated with the energy that they contained behind them. I risked a glance behind me and found that I was the only one standing there. I looked at the guard closest to the door, whose expression was completely void of all emotion. I took a hesitant step closer and he heaved the door open for me to walk through.

My eyes widened in absolute rapture at the scene in front of me. The doors opened to a grand ballroom, lit brighter with more candles than I had ever seen and swirling with all the colors of the rainbow reflecting off the dresses of the ladies. Beyond the ballroom, it looked as if a whole wall had been opened up and it flowed into a large courtyard, lit romantically by moonlight and candles and adorned with fountains and shrubs and statues. Once I had taken in as much of the scenery as I could from my vantage point, I began to focus on the faces of those nearest to me. I had never seen so many people in my life, and I was suddenly acutely aware that every eye was staring directly at me.

Chapter 19

Panic was the first thing I felt. I had forgotten about Victoria in those few seconds I had taken to absorb the grandeur of the ball. She could be anywhere. She could be watching me this second. But my fear became embarrassment as I looked more closely at the unfamiliar faces of the people staring at me. The older women had expressions of wonder and astonishment. The younger women's expressions were closer to envy and some even fury. The men gazed at me with expressions I did not recognize but didn't exactly want to.

Suddenly a person was at my side, a breathless person who was offering me a drink from a glistening glass tray. I didn't have to look to see that it was Will, but I turned and smiled at him and whispered a thank you. We both knew I was thanking him for more than just the drink.

Will was the picture of dignity and professionalism as he subtly led me to a safe corner. Most of the eyes of the crowd returned to what they had been looking at before I had come through the doors, but for some reason I had certainly made an impression, an unwelcome impression considering I had hoped to slip into the ball undetected.

"I didn't want to be noticed," I whispered when we were safely away from peering eyes.

"Impossible," he said in a teasing, yet admiring, tone.

I smiled and blushed. I scanned the crowd again and saw that a man in an official-looking uniform was staring at me. I recognized him as one of the men who had noticed me when I entered the room, and I ducked my head. I watched him stride away past me, a sense of purpose in his step.

"Do you know who he is?" I whispered to Will. "He looks important."

"That's Sir Thomas. He's one of the prince's most trusted advisors." Then he added, "He's an excellent horseman. He prefers a dressage saddle."

I laughed, surprised and impressed. Of course I knew Will was here every day, but it was illuminating actually seeing him here, realizing how much he knew about this royal world and the people in it.

"Relax. I'll be watching as best I can," Will said. People had been taking drinks from off his tray and it was now filled with empty glasses. "I better go refill this. If you stay in this corner, you should be safe for a few minutes until I get back."

Will strode quickly away from me and I again felt horribly guilty about the position I was putting him in. He had left his earlier duties at the stables to bring me to the ball, temporarily stealing a carriage in the process, and now he was worrying about keeping me safe and happy as well as keeping his job.

With this realization, I was determined to take more responsibility for my own safety and happiness at the ball. I wouldn't let Will risk his job for me. I had eyes; I could look for Victoria. I had feet, and I would dance. Leaving the security of the wall that my back had been attached to, I stepped out into the crowd.

Almost immediately, I spied the village doctor, but not before he saw me. He was already walking in my direction, a look of concern across his face and a small triangular sand-wich in his hand. I glanced subtly to my left then right, hoping to escape somehow. I was very fond of the doctor, but he was just the sort of person who might innocently mention to Victoria that I was at the ball. But we had made eye contact, and there was nowhere I could run.

"Ella, dear!" he said, sounding just like the sweetest grand-father I wish I had known, adoration in his eyes. "You look absolutely stunning. I wish your father were here to see you. He would be bursting with pride."

"Thank you, doctor. I'm so glad you could get away for the evening." My voice quivered and my smile was tense and forced. I hoped he didn't notice.

"Yes, it is nice to spend some time out with my wife and daughters. Besides, everyone in the kingdom is here anyway." He smiled and then a dark look passed over his features. "Including some who shouldn't be here."

I gulped and a cold sweat broke out on my neck. He knew. He was going to tell Victoria. I opened my mouth to plead with him but no words would come.

"No, no. Don't try to explain," he said, waving a hand in the air. "I've always known Victoria would do whatever she felt like doing, whether I told her to or not. But that stub-born woman should be in bed!"

I hoped my sigh was inaudible, but my relief made me giddy. My smile relaxed and became genuine. "There was no keeping her home. She loves a good party." I paused, hoping I could say this tactfully. "But, doctor, would you be so kind as to not mention to her that you saw me? She hasn't seen my dress yet and I wanted to surprise her."

He nodded and winked conspiratorially, and I felt my heart slow to a regular rhythm for the first time that night.

***

THE CROWD WAS A THICK, WARM WALL AROUND ME AS I timidly walked forward, no destination in mind. I tried to be casual as I scanned the faces for Victoria, or anyone I knew who would mention to Victoria that I was there. But these were all the faces of strangers, most likely from other villages in the kingdom.

With absolutely no warning, my way to nowhere in particular was blocked by a tall man. A very tall man. He was more than a foot taller than me and I had to crane my neck to see his face. He had a huge smile with huge teeth to match and outrageously wavy hair the color of strawberries in summer. I smiled as kindly as I could at this towering man obstructing my path and his smile became miraculously wider.

"Miss, you are the prettiest little thing I have ever seen in my life," the man said as he held out his hand for mine. Not knowing what else to do, I lifted my hand, and he bowed over it and kissed it. I wished desperately that I had at least one pair of gloves. I would have gone a few days without food to avoid feeling some strange man's thick lips on my skin. My hand had never been kissed by a stranger (and it wasn't an altogether pleasant experience), but he was nice enough and I decided to relax. It wasn't his fault I didn't have gloves . . . or experience.

"May I have the next dance?" he asked, looking deeply into my eyes. It took me a moment to realize that he was trying to be charming and I didn't want to hurt his feelings, but I was concerned about being conspicuous, twirling around where anyone's eyes could see me. On the other hand, I had also promised myself that I would have a good time, so I agreed to the dance.

He offered me his arm and I had to reach higher than I thought possible to link mine through his. As we walked to the dance floor, my panic returned. The floor was absolutely exposed with hundreds of people all around it. I stopped abruptly, pulling my partner to an awkward stop. He looked down at me questioningly, hurt evident in his eyes. He must have thought I had changed my mind, and perhaps I had. At that moment, I spotted Will across the floor from us, a tray in his hand. He looked at me and nodded with a smile, indicating that it was safe. I sighed in relief . . . and a small amount of dread, when I realized I was about to dance for the first time in years. I hoped my dancing lessons from my childhood would come back to help me now.

The tall man, who I had learned was named Frederick, put his arm securely around my waist and I stretched as high as I could to try to reach his shoulder with my left hand. I had to settle for just above the elbow. The blood immediately started rushing out of my arm and I prayed the dance would be a short one. But I smiled up at him, and he looked like he would burst with joy.

The music started and I recognized it as a waltz. For the first time since Victoria sold Father's violin, I heard the hauntingly beautiful resonance of a violin as the musicians started playing, and I felt like my father was there with me. I thought I could remember exactly how the violin sounded, but hearing it again made me realize that my faded memory of the sound was weak and hollow compared to experiencing it in real life. I savored the sound so I could take it with me and make it last until the next time I would be able to hear it, hoping that there would be a next time.

Frederick smiled down at me and moved forward and my feet automatically moved backward with him. It was thrilling when the steps came back to me effortlessly as we flowed around the dance floor. I was pleasantly surprised to find that Frederick was an excellent dancer; I had been afraid his long arms and legs would get all tangled up once we started moving, but he was surprisingly graceful. I beamed up at him, absolutely immersed in the joy of the moment. I caught a glimpse of Will and saw a look of pride and awe on his face. I couldn't contain the ecstatic smile that lit my face. This was worth any risk I was taking.

The music ended and the crowd stopped their twirling to applaud the talented musicians, and I joined in wholeheartedly. The tingling in my arm had increased and then abated as I lowered my arm and the blood rushed back to my fingers. As Frederick turned to me, clearly preparing to ask for the next dance, a gloved hand patted his shoulder from behind and Frederick's smile disappeared. Frederick was so tall I couldn't even see the head of the person behind him. Frederick reluctantly turned to face the gentleman standing behind him—Roger Wallace.

My stomach twisted up in knots as I remembered how he had spoken to me in town. I glared at him and started to turn away. How dare he assume he could ask me to dance?

"Miss Blakeley, if anyone gets to dance with you, it should be the one who learned with you, don't you agree?" Roger said. His smile looked like he had practiced it in the mirror for hours.

I sighed. I had endured much worse than this. One dance wouldn't kill me.

"As long as you don't throw mud at me afterward," I said, shaking my finger at him in mock rebuke.

"*Moi? Jamais! Vous êtes trop belle.*" Why was he speaking French to me? We didn't take French lessons together. I looked away from Roger as he continued to unnecessarily speak French to me, spittle flying out of his mouth, and I thanked Frederick for a lovely dance. His smile returned, though it was now touched with unabashed envy.

Roger continued to speak French, and from what I could tell he was saying that he was glad I had bought myself a new dress and that I really was the most beautiful girl in the kingdom. He placed himself in front of me, and I reluctantly put my hand on his upper arm, slightly grateful for the relief after Frederick's height, though I quickly learned I would have taken an aching arm over the close proximity of Roger's face. He wrapped his arm so tightly around me I could barely breathe, unless I wanted to breathe his own breath coming out of his open mouth, which I most certainly did not.

I had been wrong. This dance was going to kill me.

He was so close to my face that his two eyes became blurred into one giant eye that refused to look anywhere else or even blink. It would have been funny if it hadn't been so uncomfortable and unbelievably annoying. I tried to be polite at first, but soon I was pushing against him to get some air and to try to turn his one eye back into two.

"Mr. Wallace," I gasped. "I . . . can't . . . breathe."

"Oh, I have taken your breath away, have I?" He chuckled and I continued to push against him.

It was more like a wrestling match than a waltz. He never backed off, but he did seem a little surprised by my strength. He might have been surprised to learn that just this morning his dainty dance partner had pulled a stubborn cow out from the barn to the pasture and had carried two large gallons of milk to the house, one in each hand. Maybe Victoria really did know I was at the ball, and she sent Roger to come dance with me as my punishment.

When the music ended, Roger did not let go, even to let me applaud. His face was inches from mine. I turned my head so I could catch my breath. He leaned in toward my face, his lips in a ridiculous pucker.

"That will be quite enough of that," a familiar voice said. Will sounded both extremely irritated and extremely entertained at the same time. He placed his hand on Roger's chest and pushed him roughly away from me. Then Will not so subtly squeezed his way in between me and my suddenly furious dance partner. Roger stumbled backward, trying not to trip over his own feet. I refused to thank Roger for the dance—or whatever that was—but I did thank Will out of deepest gratitude. Past Will's shoulder, I could see Roger stomp off angrily in the direction of the courtyard.

Will laughed. "What a detestable scoundrel."

"Do you know Roger well?" I asked, a little surprised.

"I don't need to know him to know exactly what he is." Will smiled. We both laughed. Will wrapped his arm around my waist and I placed my hand in his. He had never officially asked me to dance, it just happened.

"How did you know it was all right for me to come out and dance?" I asked, my eyes scanning the crowd again.

"Our dear Victoria and her delightful daughters are talking with some friends in the courtyard. Victoria is sitting on a bench looking like she'll fall over dead any second and the wicked sisters are flirting ostentatiously with any man who looks at them. They tried it on me for half a second until they realized who I was and they glowered at me like they had just seen a skunk in a suit . . . a handsome skunk in a suit." He winked and laughed out loud.

I felt instant relief. They were as far away from me as they could possibly be. I smiled up at Will and saw that he was already smiling down at me, the same look of admiration in his eyes. He was such a wonderful dancer. I didn't even have to think about the steps or worry if he would run me over or try to wrestle with me on the dance floor. It was effortless.

I was about to ask him when and where he had learned to dance, but then I noticed that he wasn't wearing his suit coat. My guilt returned, knowing that it was probably against the rules for the servants to dance with the guests and he had to be inconspicuous.

"Will, I don't want you to take any more risks for me. I would feel horrible if you were to get in trouble for helping me."

Will shrugged. "How else was I supposed to give you

the latest news? It doesn't look like there will be a break in dance partners. There's already a line behind me."

I peered over Will's shoulder and indeed saw a large group of men staring at me. In the group I saw the man whom Will had pointed out as the prince's advisor. I thought it odd that he would be standing there in the middle of my not-so-secret admirers. But something told me he wasn't waiting in line for a dance.

I didn't notice that the music had ended until Will stopped dancing. He was looking down at me, still holding me as if we were dancing. I couldn't seem to find the willpower to let go of him. I was suddenly terrified to be left alone while that man stared at me. All I could figure was that Victoria was behind it somehow. Will didn't seem ready to let go of me either, but my determined crowd of devotees descended on us. He gave my hand a little squeeze.

"You're safe," Will whispered as he stepped back, and I was instantly bombarded by potential dance partners. They were trying to appear attractive to me, while also subtly nudging the nearest contender away with their elbows.

Before they could reach me, however, I felt someone gently tap my shoulder from behind. I spun around and saw a lovely woman with soft brown eyes and a glowing smile. Without saying a word, the woman held her arms out to me and pulled me into a gentle embrace. I stood there stunned and then embraced her back. For some reason it didn't feel awkward at all, holding this woman who I'd never met before.

Without letting go, the woman said, "You look so like your mother, my dear." She pulled back and gazed at me. "I was at your parents' wedding and I would recognize that gown anywhere. It was all anyone could talk about for months after." She laughed. "I'm sorry I never introduced myself. I am Ruth Haywood. I grew up with your mother in Milton. Eleanor and I were the dearest of friends."

Her eyes began to glisten in the candlelight and, in response, mine did too. I was too stunned to speak, but I felt closer to this sweet woman than I had ever felt to any other woman in my life.

"When you walked through those doors," her voice trembled with emotion, "I thought your mother had appeared in the form of an angel." She smiled. "She always did enjoy a good ball." Her smile grew as she glanced around us. "She could gather quite a crowd too." She subtly nodded her silvery head in the direction of my eager, and increasingly impatient, admirers.

Ruth started to pull back but paused as my face fell and I clung to her.

"I don't want to take any more of your time, dear. But please come and visit me sometime. I should like to reminisce with you, if you wouldn't mind enduring an old woman's babblings."

Hot tears spilled over my cheeks. "I would love that more than you know," I said with a thick voice. She affectionately wiped my tears with her soft fingers as I still clung to her arms. She then gave me the name and location of her house, and I promised to come and visit as soon as I could. We embraced one more time, and I had to force myself to let go.

I was wearing my mother's wedding dress. I didn't think this night could be any more magical. I looked down once more to see my gown again in this new light. I heard someone clear their throat and I remembered my eager audience behind me. I took a breath to compose myself, wiped my cheeks, and turned around to find Sir Thomas inches from my face. I gasped and stepped back, but his face turned apologetic when he realized he had startled me. He held out his arm and I automatically placed mine on his. I knew I could not refuse.

"Please, come with me." We walked forward and the crowd parted before us, all eyes were once again on me.

Chapter 20

My heart pounded as we walked out into the courtyard . . . and closer to Victoria. I remembered Victoria's threat that she would have me removed from the palace if she discovered I had come, and I knew that would only be the beginning of my punishment. I assumed that I was in the process of being thrown out of the ball by this man, but I couldn't understand why we were moving away from the entrance. Perhaps there was another way to exit the palace, perhaps through a dungeon where I would be punished for my treachery.

My imagination ran wild, and I was grateful that Sir Thomas had gloves on, because my hands were slick with sweat and I refused to dry them on this dress. My glass slippers clinked quietly against the stone, and as soft as the sound was, I wished I could stop and take them off so I wouldn't attract any more attention to myself.

The farther we walked, the farther the fear fled that Victoria had anything to do with this. Sir Thomas was very professional, and it didn't seem like he was taking me to be punished. The walk went on and on, and I wondered if I should make polite conversation with my guide. I glanced up at him sideways under my lashes. He smiled kindly at me but made no move to say anything. I decided to remain silent.

The crowd thinned and soon there was no one but Sir Thomas and me. I had never been alone with any man before, except for Will, but Will was a friend. This man was a stranger and he was leading me off into the darkness. A part of me told me I should run away, but there was another part of me that was strangely curious as to where we were going and why it was me he was taking there.

I was suddenly aware of another set of footsteps besides mine—a woman's footsteps. They were quick and I could hear the soft clink of a heel. I had been wrong. Victoria knew I was here and was going to punish me. I tried to reign in my terror as I imagined Victoria suddenly appearing from behind the wall of bushes, but I was stunned to see Jane Emerson emerging out from behind them instead. Jane hadn't seen me yet, and I was too surprised to see her that I forgot that I should be hiding from her.

Jane had a small smile on her lips, her hand placed over her heart and a blush that was obvious, even in the moonlight. She was brought out of her reverie when she saw me walking with Sir Thomas. She stopped instantly and her face displayed so many emotions it was almost a spasm. Her first reaction was surprise, followed quickly by embarrassment, replaced by confusion, and then she finally settled with accusation.

I couldn't imagine what Jane was doing out here all alone, so far from anyone else, but I didn't think to ask. Similarly, she probably couldn't imagine why I was there at the ball and not sick with madness at home as she had most likely been told. I would have given her some explanation, but I was too preoccupied with the way her eyes narrowed into slits and the expression on her face that looked undoubtedly like resentment, as if I had betrayed her somehow. We passed each other in silence and it hurt more than I ever thought possible that this girl, who had been my closest friend a week ago, had somehow become more like an enemy.

All thoughts of Jane were pushed out of my mind when Sir Thomas led me to a wide, open space. I marveled at all the beautifully manicured shrubs and the intoxicating aroma of the countless blossoms hanging from planters all around the garden. There were intricately carved stone benches spaced about every thirty feet lining the garden, and dozens of statues of elegant birds with long, graceful necks that I had never seen before.

All these details I took in in a matter of seconds. The main sight that caught my attention, and held it, was that of a silhouette of a man about one hundred feet away. He was facing away from me, standing in front of a low stone wall, his hands clasped behind him, his back straight, his head held high. This could only be one person.

My guide gently cleared his throat and I looked at him. He glanced down pointedly at his arm, and I laughed nervously and let go of him. My hand ached from clinging to his arm so tightly and I stretched my fingers and glanced up at him apologetically. He smiled in understanding and dropped his arm. Gesturing to the man with his other arm, he said in a regal voice, "His Royal Highness, Prince Kenton." He bowed deeply and was gone before I could exhale.

Chapter 21

I STOOD ALONE IN THE MOONLIGHT. I WASN'T SURE IF I WAS expected to wait for the prince to come to me or if I was supposed to go and meet him. After a moment of neither one of us moving, I stepped forward. The tinkling of my footsteps was the only sound in the stillness and I felt terribly self-conscious as it echoed through the otherwise silent garden.

I slowed to a stop when I was about ten feet away from him. Not knowing if there was any protocol on how close one could stand to a prince, I kept my distance and waited. Out of habit from dealing with Victoria, I waited to be spoken to before I allowed myself to speak.

The prince slowly turned to face me, his hands still clasped behind him. He was absurdly handsome, even more so in the moonlight than at midday when I had last seen him. A satisfied smile touched his full lips as he looked me over.

"You're a brave one," he said in a low, smooth voice as he stepped closer to me. "The last girl stood back there for five minutes before she came over to me."

I found my voice, though it was breathless and trembling. "I don't blame her." I didn't exactly feel like defending Jane at the moment, but I suddenly felt a surge of pity for my friend.

Poor Jane must have been in complete terror standing there alone in the dark, wondering what she was supposed to do. "I thought I was being taken out here to be executed." I surprised myself by laughing a free, easy laugh. Perhaps I was giddy with relief that I was going to leave the ball with my head still attached to my body.

He looked at me for a moment with an amused look on his face and then laughed with me.

I bowed my head to hide my flaming cheeks and curtsied as low as I could with my billowing skirts swirling around me. "It's lovely to meet you, Your Highness."

"Please . . . call me Your Majesty. It's much more . . . majestic," the prince said.

I blushed even more deeply as I opened my mouth to form a clumsy apology, but it couldn't make it past my dry throat.

The prince laughed again. "I'm so sorry. I should leave the joke-telling to you." He chuckled and relaxed his stance, placing his hands in his pockets. "My name is Kenton. I would say that you may call me that, but I think we'd better settle for Prince Kenton. My parents want me to keep at least some distance between me and the commoners." He rolled his eyes as he said the last word. He smiled down at me, seeming to try to make me feel more comfortable. "But you're anything but common, so I don't think we have to worry about that."

I flushed to my hairline and I tried to command my heart to slow down. It disobeyed, naturally. As I silently beseeched my cheeks to return to their normal color, I tried to reconcile this prince with the prince I had first seen in town and who I had seen driving through the countryside. The man who stood before me seemed very different from the man who had climbed up onto the fountain in the village square and enthusiastically invited us all to the ball. That prince was larger than life, flirtatious, and almost too much to take in—probably trying to excite the crowd. The prince from the countryside was captivating and seemed almost mystified. This prince was, so far, very charming.

"Come this way," he said. I followed him to stand in front of the wall where he had been waiting for me. I gasped when I saw that this was not only a wall, but a balcony from which we could see the entire kingdom blanketed in moonlight.

Far off in the distance nestled behind the hills was Lytton, and beyond its borders was the sea. I hadn't been there since I was a little girl, but I could almost smell the sticky, salty air and feel the grainy sand in between my toes. To my right was Maycott, my little village. I could see the hill that Father and I rode horses on when I was a little girl. Beyond the hill, there was a thick patch of tall trees and I knew that in the middle of it was the glassy pond, and just beyond it was Ashfield. If the sun had been up, I probably could have made out a tiny tower in the distance that was my bedroom. I looked far to my left and saw the very edges of Milton, the village my mother grew up in. My whole world, my past and my present, was right in front of my eyes in one sweeping glance. I wondered if I could also see my future from where I stood.

I didn't know how long I had been staring out over the kingdom and laughed a little at myself for being so preoccupied with the landscape when I was standing in the presence of a prince.

"What's so amusing?" the prince asked. He was standing startlingly close and I jumped a little.

I turned to face him but took an instinctive step back because of his close proximity. "Please forgive me, Your Highness. I suppose it's difficult for me to look away from beautiful things."

"I know exactly what you mean," he said, gazing deeply into my eyes.

I blushed furiously and my rebellious heart pounded in my chest. I was sure the prince could hear it, which made me blush deeper. I took another faltering step back.

"Please forgive me. I . . . I . . ."

"You keep asking forgiveness, but you've done nothing wrong." He smiled kindly. "You look like you need to sit down. Come with me." He offered me his arm and I hesitatingly raised mine and linked it through his.

We walked toward the closest bench. He gestured for me to sit and he sat beside me. I pulled my arm out of his, but the prince grabbed my hand instead. I was shocked by his boldness. The only man close to my age I ever interacted with was Will and he had always kept a careful distance between us, or I had.

I looked down at our hands and was relieved once again that the prince was wearing gloves so he couldn't feel the moisture on my hands. I made a silent note to myself that the next time I sneaked out of my house in a stolen carriage to go to a forbidden ball to meet a prince, I would be sure to wear gloves.

"You are quite bold, Your Highness," I remarked. I knew I was not calling him Prince Kenton as he had requested, but I just couldn't make the words come.

"And I suspect you are quite reserved," he guessed.

I smiled. "I live a quiet life in my own little world."

"Tell me about your world," he whispered, scooting closer to me as if anticipating a marvelously fascinating story.

I was not expecting this. "For one thing, princes don't hold my hand in my little world." We laughed and I glanced down at our entwined hands, trying to grasp where I really was and who I was with. The prince reached out his other hand and seized my other hand too, as if to emphasize that I truly was in a very different world at the moment and that a prince was very willingly holding my hands. I wondered what he would think of my world and what he would do if he knew the hands he now held milked cows and plucked chickens. I decided I wasn't ready to tell him or if I ever would be. "Perhaps you should tell me about yours first."

He waved a hand carelessly through the air. "I'm sure you know all there is to know. Crowns, extravagant clothes, servants, expectations, traveling, diplomacy, balls." He returned his hand to mine.

"Don't you enjoy your life?" I was surprised I had asked such a forward question of a prince. Who was I to ask if he enjoyed his privileged life?

He didn't seem to be bothered by my question or think me impertinent. "I suppose it would be dishonest to say that I don't enjoy certain things about this life. But I can say that I definitely do not enjoy the monotony of it. I was born into this life and it's all I've ever known, which is why I'm curious about your life. Are you going to tell me about it now?" He raised his eyebrows and smiled, indicating he had not been fooled by my evasiveness.

I looked away from the prince and back at the landscape. He didn't seem to be in a rush, so I gave myself time to think. I didn't know what to tell him, or how much, or why it even mattered. He was simply curious about how I, a commoner, lived. He was the one who had invited the villagers so he could see how the people in his kingdom lived their lives. I decided to tell him the truth.

I turned back to face him and opened my mouth to speak, but was silenced by the prince's expression.

"I have traveled the world for most of my life." He paused, struggling for words. "And I have never seen anyone or anything as beautiful as you."

He raised his steady hand and placed it gently against my jaw, turning my face up to his. This was no awkward, half-drunk dance partner's attempt at a kiss. This was the prince and I suspected he knew exactly what he was doing. I also suspected that he had never been refused. Until now.

"Your Highness," I whispered. His eyes flew open in surprise, but his face stayed where it was, bewilderment and curiosity in his eyes. "You don't even know me," I said. "I hope you don't think me rude, but no one has ever kissed me before and, well, I'm terrified." I remembered what Will had said to me—that I was never his to kiss. Did all men feel that way? Was the prince claiming me with his kiss? I went on, feeling more confident. "I didn't know that I was being brought up here to kiss a prince. And if this is some kind of test, I'm fairly certain that I just failed. Please forgive me."

The prince listened to my speech, his face turning from slightly irritated, to confused, then to something that looked like astonishment. He dropped his hand and pulled back. "No, it is I who have failed. Yes, I wanted to meet you and get to know you, but I have forgotten myself. It is I who need to ask your forgiveness."

"I doubt I'm in any position to forgive a prince," I said, laughing nervously. But something he said had caught my attention. "Why did you want to meet me? There are dozens, hundreds, of women here. Why me?"

For the first time, the prince looked embarrassed. His one hand that still held mine gently dropped it in my lap and he went to stand at the balcony. I sat silently, watching from the bench, and waited for him to speak.

"I have been traveling the world for years now, searching for the next queen of this kingdom," he said to the empty air. "I have met countless women and I have been deeply dissatisfied with all of them. There is a certain princess my parents want me to marry, but she is a horrible person. She is hateful and cruel and selfish and spoiled."

For a moment I wondered if he was talking about Victoria

and I was grateful he was turned away from me and couldn't see my smile.

"But she is a princess and with our union, we would gain an ally in her kingdom." He shook his head, apparently displeased with that reason for marrying someone. "The king and queen know how much I detest the woman they want me to marry, and honestly, they don't like her much either—princess or not. So we came to an agreement that if I could find someone suitable to marry, someone who could someday be a queen, then I could marry that girl instead. She could be anyone I chose, from any walk of life. But," he said, pausing, "according to our law, I have to marry her before my twenty-fifth birthday."

"Isn't your birthday coming soon?" I asked. I felt foolish for not knowing the exact date. I was sure we had some sort of celebration to mark his birthday each year, but I had never paid much attention.

He turned back around to face me. "Three days," he replied, a sense of finality in his voice.

I tried not to gape at him. "Forgive me, Your Highness, but if you are supposed to be married in three days, why are you only now bringing women here to talk to them and meet them . . . and kiss them?" I grinned. "Or try to."

He heard the smugness in my voice and laughed lightly. "I know it sounds terrible, and I promise I haven't been trying to kiss every girl who has come to meet me." He paused and smiled at me. "Just you. I guess you could say you swept me off my feet." He looked down at me and returned to sit down next to me.

It still didn't explain why I was brought here in the first place. Why weren't all the women at the ball lined up and brought to him? "Why was I brought here?" I asked bluntly.

"You looked like a princess," the prince said simply.

Chapter 22

I SURPRISED US BOTH BY THROWING MY HEAD BACK AND laughing out loud. "Because I looked like a princess?" I now knew the role that Sir Thomas had to play—to search the ball for the woman who looked like she could become the next queen. "I'm honored, Your Highness, but just because I look like a princess today doesn't mean I look like this all the time. It wouldn't be very practical. And just because someone thinks I might look like a princess doesn't mean I would make a good one." I took a breath and continued, "Why did you wait so long to look for a wife? Why didn't you have the ball a year ago? Two years ago?" I had a dozen other questions but stopped myself. It was obvious the prince had never been spoken to that way, and I guessed by the astonished way he was staring at me, he wasn't pleased about it. I ducked my head in shame.

He gaped at me for a moment. "Thank you," he said abruptly, again clasping my hands in both of his. "That is the first time anyone has ever been completely open with me. That was exhilarating. But to answer your many questions: Yes, it does seem ridiculous waiting so long, but I suppose I didn't really know what I wanted until recently. I'm bored with this life and living with people who have only known this life. It makes us spoiled and uninteresting. We only see what's happening to us and we worry and talk about trivial things. That's why I wanted to be able to marry anyone I wanted. A princess or a servant. A duchess or a dairy maid. I get so few choices in my life, and I wanted to make this one."

I nodded in understanding. "I don't blame you for wanting to choose who you marry, and I admire you for being willing to marry anyone. But if I may warn you, one can become quite spoiled in any sort of life." I thought of Victoria and how she somehow demanded living a life of royalty even in the midst of our painfully obvious poverty. "Anyone could become bored and frustrated with their life if they haven't figured out how to see the good in it." I fell silent and took a breath and smiled, feeling a sense of clarity. "Your life and my life are not that different." I ducked my head again, abruptly ashamed of what sounded like a chastisement of the prince.

"But is it a bad thing to want to improve your life or to seek for a better one?" he said, lifting my head up again with his finger under my chin.

I knew why he asked the question and I thought I knew the answer—until right then. Here I was at the palace, having escaped out of my own life for a night to see what it would be like to live another one. I didn't think it was a bad thing, though I had struggled with my worthiness to even experience it. But now that I was here, I couldn't say if one life was necessarily better than the other.

"No, there's nothing wrong with seeking a different life, as long as that life will make you truly happy." I smiled when I realized how simple the answer really was. "Different isn't always better."

The prince stared at me for so long, I wanted to drop my eyes, but I held them steady and looked back into his.

He slowly shook his head back and forth as if in complete astonishment. He glanced down when something caught his eye.

"Look at that tiny slipper! And your tiny feet! I've never seen such tiny feet!" he cried.

"They were my mother's," I replied with a smile. "The slippers, I mean, not my feet. Well, maybe those, too." I laughed.

"Please tell me about yourself," the Prince pleaded. "How have I never seen you before tonight? I know I don't spend much time out of the palace walls, but even so, I don't know how someone like you could have possibly escaped my notice."

His words stung me slightly and my pain gave me courage. "Actually, Your Highness, you have seen me twice before tonight, but I didn't look like I do right now. You saw me in the square on the day you invited us all to the ball. You saw me from your carriage on Sunday as you drove by."

Recognition was dawning on his face mingled with denial.

I sighed but with resolution. "I am a servant in my own home. I wear the same ragged dress every day. I don't own a pair of gloves because I sold them all to pay for food to feed my stepmother, my stepsisters, and myself. We have also sold all of my father's prized horses, most of the furniture, tapestries, vases, china, and animals. My bedroom is in the tallest tower so that I can be as far away from my stepmother as possible because if she sees me, she will find some fault with me, for which I will most likely be whipped. I wake before dawn and go to bed after dark, usually sleeping on the hearth because I'm too exhausted to climb up to my tower.

"My mother died shortly after I was born, and my father died when I was ten. The girl who I had thought was my closest friend turned me into a rival almost as soon as the ball was announced. She was the shy girl who you met right before me. I was forbidden to come tonight by my stepmother and she took every possible means to make it impossible for me to come." I absently reached up to touch the twist at the nape of my neck. "And if she finds out I'm here, with you especially, I will be severely punished."

My voice softened. "I have one true friend in the world, and that's all I need."

I paused, but the prince waited for me to continue.

"I love my home. It is a part of who I am. I love my cow, Lucy, and my chicken, Mary. I love my garden and taking care of it and watching things grow. I love the forest I can see out my window. I work hard to keep my home beautiful and clean, and I take joy and pride in my work. My body is strong and my hands are roughened with work. I can make meals out of nothing. I sweep and scrub and polish and dust. And I'm not ashamed of it. I have a purpose. I know who I am and why I do what I do."

My eyes blazed as I spoke, not out of anger, but with an intensity I had never felt before. I had always known why I slaved in my house every day, but I had never spoken it out loud. I realized how much I truly wanted to do it. Not just because I had promised to and not just because everyone was depending on me, but because I loved it and it gave my life meaning.

While I spoke, it felt like I was talking more to myself than to the prince, reassuring myself that I had value that had nothing to do with what I was wearing.

I was so involved in my little speech that I didn't realize the prince was staring back at me, his eyes troubled, his mouth slightly open, and his head slowly shaking back and forth.

"That couldn't have been you I saw on the road that day. That girl was . . . dirty and sad. She . . . she had long hair."

"Yes, I was dirty and sad that day. My hair was long, but it is now short because I had to sell it to buy back these things I'm wearing because they were stolen from me."

He glanced up at my hair, completely baffled. "Sell it?" he whispered. It was as if he had never heard of such a thing. He reached up a hand to gently stroke my hair, then returned his hand to mine. "Well, don't worry. It will grow again," he said with a small smile.

I didn't look away as the prince continued to study me—my face, my short hair, my bare hands, my dress, my slippers. I was caught off guard, though, when he placed both his hands on my neck and leaned in and kissed me. My eyes flew open in surprise. It didn't matter that I had never kissed anyone before; I was in capable hands. He held me tight and my eyes closed and the world disappeared. I didn't know what this kiss meant to him, and I didn't get the chance to ask him.

He pulled back and his eyes were almost fiercely ardent. "I've only just met you, but I've never been more fascinated by anyone in my entire life. I can't imagine marrying anyone else but you." He brushed his lips across my cheek and next to my ear and whispered, "I love you." He grasped a lock of hair that had had fallen loose and tucked it behind my ear. "I want you to be my bride. You'll never have to work another day in your life. I want to give you everything: gowns, jewels, horses, carriages . . ." Something seemed to suddenly dawn on him and he laughed softly. "And I don't even know your name."

It took me longer than it should have for me to realize that this was when I was supposed to tell him my name. I was still in shock from just having been kissed for the first time, and by a prince, no less, and he had just said he loved me and wanted to marry me.

He placed a finger gently under my chin and leaned in and whispered in my ear. "Your name, beautiful lady?" He brushed his lips across my cheek.

My voice was caught in my throat. I would love to tell him my name, if I could only remember it.

But something didn't feel right. My mind was fuzzy and I was terribly confused. I couldn't even put into words what I was feeling and I was angry at myself for being so ridiculous. I looked back into the prince's eyes as he waited patiently for me to answer.

He had just called me beautiful. He had just told me he loved me. What was wrong with me? Why did I feel like escaping?

I started to pull free of his hands. He looked down at our entwined hands with a look of utter disbelief.

"I'm sorry. I have to go," I said, barely believing my own words, but feeling that they were the right ones.

Suddenly, the prince clasped my hands tighter just as they were about to slip free of his. He held me close and then his lips were at my ear. "I'm sorry I scared you. Please don't go. I love you." Those words again. They were beautiful words, but they felt so out of place.

I looked up into his perfect face, still reeling from this rapid turn of events. "I'm sorry," I whispered. I pulled free out of his hands and began to run as fast as I possibly could.

I felt his arms drop lifelessly to his sides once I was out of his grasp. He appeared to be as astonished as I was that I was running away from him as fast as my slippers would allow. Abruptly, he seemed to come to his senses.

"Stop her!" His voice rang through the empty garden from behind me. I heard his footsteps far in the distance, but I had a head start.

Somewhere in the flight, my glass slipper got caught in a wide crack in the stone and slipped off my foot. I didn't even pause as I ran into the night, my dress trailing behind me.

Chapter 23

I RACED OUT OF THE COURTYARD, THROUGH THE BALL-room, into the palace, and out the enormous front doors. People looked at me with outrage as I pushed past them, but I kept running. I didn't even care if Victoria saw me; I just had to get home. Once I was away from the prince, I probably would have felt safe to simply walk away from the palace, but the fact that I was being chased forced me to flee. Luckily, the guards I passed had no idea that they were supposed to be stopping me yet. They just exchanged looks of confusion, but it wouldn't be long before they chased after me too. I fled down the great front steps and kept running until I reached the iron gate near the bottom of the hill. The guards opened it for me, trying not to show any emotion, but were unable to hide their bafflement as a girl without a carriage ran past them.

I only paused once as I slipped off my one slipper and grasped it tightly in my hand. I continued down the sloping hill of the palace and into the middle of town where I had first seen the prince. There wasn't a soul in sight, but in the distance toward the castle I heard voices calling out, mingled with the sound of quick footsteps and horses' hooves pounding the ground. I grabbed my skirts and held them up above my ankles so they wouldn't slow me down, ignored the dirt road, and dashed into the woods that led more quickly, and discreetly, to home. I felt branches pull at my gown and rocks and twigs scrape my bare feet.

I didn't know what was driving me forward more—the need to run away from the palace, or the need to be home. I couldn't think about the prince. It was too confusing, too much to take in in such a short amount of time, too impossible to be true.

I burst through the trees, leaves and dirt stuck to the bottom of my bloody feet, and I did not stop running until I reached the front drive of Ashfield. It was then that I seemed to come back down to reality.

I had snuck out. I was supposed to be at home, crying in a corner. As far as I knew, Victoria didn't know I had gone to the ball. I couldn't see any candles lit inside, so perhaps I had made it home before she had. I wondered if it were possible for me to enter through the kitchen undetected.

I looked around me to make sure I hadn't been followed home. All was quiet. Deathly quiet. The tranquil loveliness of the moon from earlier in the evening had turned ghostly and cold and it sent a shiver up my back and to my bare neck. As I made my way up the long drive, I was surprised to see a carriage parked close to the house, one wheel precariously balanced on the front steps. The two horses that had pulled the carriage were huffing loudly and covered in sweat.

Victoria was home. And she had come home in a hurry. She knew I had been at the ball. There was no point in hiding from her now. With a sigh, I walked up the steps and heaved open the great oak doors. I had expected Victoria to be waiting for me, cold and formidable, at the top of the stairs, a subtle sneer on her lips. I looked up the stairs to the hall and saw the dark glow of candlelight flooding out of her open door.

Gathering all my courage, I slowly moved forward, reaching out to hold onto the warped wood of the banister and climbed up the stairs. Once I reached the landing, I stood in the open doorway of Victoria's room and took in the scene in front of me.

Victoria was on her bed on top of the quilts, still in her evening dress. Her eyes were closed and her breaths came in shallow huffs. Mabel and Cecelia were standing in the far corner of the room, glaring at me with more hatred than they ever had. It almost seemed as if they knew who I had spent the evening with and they also saw that I somehow had my gown and slippers back, or at least one slipper back, which I clutched tightly in my hand. I could feel my chopped hair brushing bluntly on top of my shoulders, but I didn't care what they thought of it.

The doctor was sitting on the edge of Victoria's bed, checking her pulse on her wrist. Now I knew who the carriage belonged to. He was staring at me through eyes filled with pity. "Ella," he said softly. "Victoria is dying. She doesn't have long. I'm so sorry, my dear."

Dying? I felt myself blink slowly, trying to grasp what he had just said. I knew she was ill, but she had been well enough to go to the ball . . . hadn't she?

He turned to face the other two girls in the corner. "I'll leave you to say good-bye to your mother, girls."

The doctor left the room and seemed surprised to see me following him. I answered the unasked question in his eyes. "I'll let them talk to her first." I said vacantly.

Once we were out of her bedroom, I collapsed in the same chair I had sat in while father lay dying in the bed across the hall. I could hear his frail voice over and over in my mind, "Take care of them. Take care of them. Take care of them."

I looked at the doctor, who was rubbing between his eyes with his fingers. "What happened tonight, doctor?"

He dropped his hand from his face and sighed. "I decided to stay near your stepmother tonight. I had told her that she should not be out of bed and I was terribly worried about her. She was sitting on a bench, searching the crowd with an almost crazed expression. I never knew what she was looking for. Then, that sweet girl Jane Emerson came and whispered something in Victoria's ear. I've never seen such anger in anyone's eyes as I did in Victoria's at that moment. She stood so swiftly that it startled everyone around her. She began to run in the direction that Jane had come from, then quite suddenly, she stopped, her knees buckled, and she fell to the ground. I rushed over to her and all she would say was, 'Ella. Ella.'"

The doctor looked at me with a penetrating gaze. He was not accusatory, but it was obvious that he was confused as to why she would be saying my name. I felt he deserved an explanation.

I swallowed hard. "Victoria forbade me from going to the ball. I disobeyed her and sneaked out after she had gone. But Jane saw me at the ball and must have told Victoria I had come after all." There was so much more to the story: my dress and slippers being stolen, Victoria's cruel words about my father, my whole week of whippings, and really my whole life of servitude to her. But that was all I said. The doctor nodded in understanding. He had seen a little of what life was like at Ashfield now and I think he knew that there was more to it than I could say.

"Well, we managed to get her home and into bed, but she hasn't spoken since the ball." He sighed, the stress of the evening sinking in.

"Thank you, Doctor. I'm grateful that you were so near to her and I'm sure Victoria is too." He smiled and patted my hands, which were resting on my lap.

Just then, Cecelia and Mabel exited Victoria's room. I

didn't know what to expect, but I shouldn't have been surprised to see two girls with dry eyes and calm faces step out of their dead, or almost dead, mother's room.

"Is she . . . ?" I asked.

Mabel shook her head with a blank look on her face.

I sighed and stood. I knew this would be the last time I ever spoke to Victoria.

Chapter 24

I WALKED THROUGH THE OPEN DOORWAY AND INTO THE consuming gloom; the darkness pressed in on me, making it difficult to breathe. I crept slowly to the foot of my stepmother's bed and drew in a labored breath. Victoria looked like a skeleton. She still had her elegant dress on and I realized that she would want to die in something extravagant, not a plain nightgown. But I also knew that Victoria did not want to die at Ashfield, no matter what she was wearing.

I reached Victoria's bedside, scarcely aware that I was moving and not knowing what compelled me to move even closer to her. The dim light from the single candle on the bedside table cast deathly shadows over her sunken cheeks, making them appear hollow. Her breathing was so shallow it made me take another unsteady breath, trying to compensate somehow.

I stood looking at my stepmother. For nearly ten years, I had trained myself not to feel too deeply, because then I might hurt too deeply. Any time I would hurt, I would only let it be a superficial feeling—not allowing it to consume me, not letting the pain in. Occasionally, I would shed a tear or two, and move on. It was necessary to my survival.

But as I gazed down at the person who could have and should have taken care of me when I had needed her most, the emotions I had been burying for so long bubbled up to the surface. I felt abandonment knowing that the person who could have grieved with me when Father died had instead brushed me aside. I felt bitterness for every time she saw the bad in me instead of the good. I felt anguish because she sought for power and control instead of empathy and love.

Then, so unexpectedly it knocked the air out from my lungs, I felt a startling and overpowering wave of pity course through my veins. What had happened in Victoria's life that had made her into such a hateful creature? Why couldn't she show real love to anyone, including her own daughters?

I realized I knew almost nothing about this woman. What were her parents like? Her childhood? Her first husband? Had he been kind? I had been pushed away every time I had tried to get to know her. She hadn't wanted to know me, and she had never allowed me to know her. But still, at this moment when Victoria's life was about to end, I felt a deep sadness for her that I knew, as soon as I felt it, would always be a part of me.

I took comfort knowing that even though Victoria had been cruel and harsh with me, I had tried my best to serve and please her. I had given, I had sacrificed, I had worked and slaved and toiled. And though it was very often fear of her that kept me from running away, there was always something deeper that kept me here.

I had promised to take care of her, and I had kept that promise.

I thought back over the countless hours I had spent brushing Victoria's long graying hair and drawing her baths; of washing and mending her clothes; of making her bed and folding her quilts; and of all the meals I had made and watching Victoria's face when she truly enjoyed it. And though she had never thanked me, it was still satisfying knowing I had pleased her. It was something that had been expected, and even ordered of me, but now I saw it as a small offering—an offering of my time and energy for the woman my father, for whatever reason, had once loved.

I suddenly knew the answer to the question I had asked myself for years. Why did Victoria's daughters seemingly care nothing for her? Why did she keep us all at a distance? She didn't treat them as coldly as she treated me, but there was still no warmth or tenderness in her eyes when she looked at her daughters. How could they leave her on her deathbed without so much as a tear? It was because they had never been taught to serve, never been taught to love or empathize. They had been taught to demand and tease and manipulate. They felt no real love for their mother because she had never loved or served them either. But I had always seen Victoria's behavior as simply vicious and heartless, and not a mask for her own pain.

My heart swelled with so much pity and sorrow that it felt like it would burst. I personally had no regrets. I knew I had done all I could. But to know that so many years of Victoria's life were wasted on vanity and pride and an unquenchable thirst for power hurt me more than any whipping ever could. And to now consider the very real possibility that she showed me only cruelty and contempt was because she most likely had been treated the same way made my pain mingle with hers. This was a pain that ran deep, a pain that had to be healed from the inside out—a pain I was actually grateful to feel in time to do something about it.

Victoria hadn't moved at all from the time I came into her room, and I didn't even know how long I had been standing there. I sat down in the chair next to the bed and reached out to take Victoria's withered hand. I was not hesitant in the least. There was no time for that.

"Victoria," I whispered. Her eyes flickered under her eyelids, and I knew she could hear me. "Victoria, I forgive you. I forgive you for any hurt you have caused me. I'm so sorry for any hurt you have known in your life. I wish that I could have known you better, that we could have been friends, but I want you to know I bear no ill will toward you. We have all done the best we could with the lot we've been given. We all have our trials, and I feel peace for you knowing that yours will soon be over, and I pray that you too will find peace."

Tears had begun to roll down my cheeks, but my voice was neither timid nor trembling. The tears fell freely and splashed onto the sheets. It felt as if a physical weight had been lifted off my shoulders, and even sitting in that stale room that was filled with sickness and death, I felt as if I were breathing fresh air for the first time in years.

I knew I could not have said these words when Victoria had been healthy and strong and domineering. They would have been met with sarcasm and antagonism. But it didn't matter. Clarity had come in these last hours that I couldn't have experienced before. And the empathy that had grown inside of me in the last few moments had rapidly evolved into something that resembled love.

I sat weeping by my stepmother's bedside when Victoria's limp and bony fingers gripped mine with a sudden fierceness. I looked up in amazement and saw a tear glisten out of the corner of Victoria's closed eye. It ran down the side of her face and into her hair.

Chapter 25

Victoria died at midnight. I felt her icy fingers release my hand, and I knew she was gone. I carefully folded her arms across her chest and kissed her forehead. I stumbled out of the room and silently closed the door behind me.

I was suddenly so weary, my limbs felt as heavy as the great marble pillars of Ashfield. I informed the doctor that Victoria was gone and we set about making the necessary arrangements. I didn't know if this was his usual role—planning the burials for his patients—but I was very grateful for the help. Victoria would be buried in the garden next to my father and mother—a thought that would have torn at my heart even an hour before. But now that my feelings had been softened toward her, it felt quite appropriate. I knew that Father would have been pleased.

Once everything had been arranged, the doctor made his preparations to leave, telling me he would notify the mortician to come and get the body. He told me to go and get some rest, that I didn't need to be awake when they came.

I walked the doctor to the door and he glanced up to the bedroom doors on the second floor. He shifted his weight and twirled his hat around in his hands.

"Your sisters are talking about leaving. Mabel received a proposal tonight."

"Of marriage?" My voice came out in a strangled whisper. I was absolutely shocked. I couldn't even imagine who it could be. I hadn't heard of her being courted by anyone.

He nodded slowly. "I'm sure she'll fill you in on all the details." He tried to smile but couldn't quite manage it. "I told your sisters I would take them to where they were going, so I'll just wait outside for them." He paused and then added gently, "Do you have anywhere to go?"

"I'm not going anywhere," I stated, perhaps a little too firmly.

"Good." His dry lips lifted slightly in an exhausted smile. I couldn't stop myself from throwing my arms around him and thanking him. He patted my back gently and kissed my cheek, then walked to his carriage and waited for my stepsisters.

After seeing the doctor out, I climbed up the stairs and stood outside my stepsisters' bedrooms. They were running back and forth from their wardrobes to their beds where they each had their travel bags on top. They were hurriedly stuffing dresses, bonnets, worn shoes, and frayed stockings into the bags. They must have hated this house just as much as Victoria had.

"You're really leaving? Now?" I asked. I didn't sound accusatory—I didn't have the energy for that. I was merely curious.

Mabel stopped her packing and looked at me with a strange combination of haughtiness and chagrin. The hint of remorse in her eyes softened all of her features and for a moment she was the stunningly beautiful little girl I had first met. Cecelia was suddenly by her side, looking at her sister as if she'd never seen her before. There was compassion in Cecelia's eyes that looked so foreign on her face I wouldn't have recognized her.

"I . . . I am to be married," Mabel said. "It wasn't supposed to be for another few months, but once they hear what has happened to mother, I'm sure it will be sooner. The Wallaces have already begged Cecelia and me to stay with them so we can plan the wedding."

"The Wallaces? Oh, not Roger Wallace, Mabel! Anyone but him. He's terrible."

"He's rich," Mabel said with a shrug. "I'm tired of being poor."

I blinked in disbelief and turned to Cecelia. "Cecelia, what about you? What will you do there once Mabel is married?"

"Roger has a rich cousin who will be coming into town for the wedding. Mrs. Wallace says he's perfect for me."

There was nothing else to say. They had it all planned out and there was nothing I could do. I wondered if they had returned to their original plan of ensnaring Roger Wallace when they realized they wouldn't be able to meet the prince tonight. And I wondered if it was Mabel who Roger strode off to after our horrible dance. I felt desperately sorry for Mabel. I didn't know if she knew what she was getting herself into, but it seemed she didn't care, which was infinitely worse. She saw an escape and she was taking it. And she was taking Cecelia with her.

We stood there in silence for a moment, and then Cecelia raised her hand and placed it on Mabel's shoulder. Mabel nodded and Cecelia smiled faintly in return. They retrieved their bags, walked down the stairs, and to the front door. Before they closed the door, they turned to look at me once more.

It was almost impossible for me to identify the expression on their faces that had always been made of stone. It looked like relief and perhaps a hint of regret.

I was stunned to silence and I stood looking at the closed

door for a long time. They had become different people in a matter of moments. I realized that they had also suffered. They had had to protect themselves too. They had learned from their mother to treat me unkindly and so I assumed that they, too, were unkind. But they did what was expected of them, just as I had. I had always been taught by my father to recognize others' suffering, but somehow I hadn't been able to see the suffering of those who were closest to me. It's true they were the reason for my own pain, but I had let it blind me into thinking that their suffering went no deeper than a sadness over a lack of new dresses and decadent food. Could they have missed their own father and their old life? I might never know. We had all worn our masks and played our roles well.

I was overwhelmed by all the awareness I was suddenly feeling. I wondered if there was anything else that was going to be revealed to me now that my mask was off.

I willed my feet forward and I climbed the long stairs up to my tower, my sanctuary. It felt like I had just lived the longest day of my life. The stairs wound endlessly upward, and it seemed like they had doubled in length as I dizzily rounded each corner. My feet were bloody and raw from running through the woods, so I placed my one slipper back on my foot to provide some protection from the slivers and knots in the wooden stairs. My bare foot was silent against the steps, but the soft clinking of my single glass slipper on my other foot reminded me that I had abandoned my shoe in my hasty escape from the palace. Grief crushed me as I realized I had lost something precious of my mother's—again. I couldn't think about that now, but I wondered vaguely, as I wearily climbed the stairs, if I would ever see it again.

I reached my door and lethargically pushed it open. My room looked exactly as I had left it, whenever it had been that I had last slept there. I wanted to feel like I was coming to a place where I could feel safe, but considering that the reason for my personal banishment was now dead, it suddenly felt pointless to be up here all alone. I longed for the large and comfortable bedroom I hadn't slept in since I was a little girl—my rightful place in this house.

With an unexpected indescribable joy, followed by a tiny twinge of guilt for feeling that joy, I realized I was now the lady of the house.

Nothing changed. The cupboards didn't magically fill with food. The cow wasn't automatically milked by anyone. No one gathered the eggs or weeded the garden. The banister wasn't sanded or repainted. The furniture that had been sold didn't miraculously reappear. Breakfast wouldn't be waiting for me on the table in the morning. My violin wasn't returned, and my hair didn't grow back. But I finally felt at home in my home.

I promised myself that I would move back to my old room the next day. But tonight, I would sleep. I pulled off my shimmering dress and replaced it with my tattered nightgown. I hung up my beautiful gown and examined it closely, looking for any signs of dirt or tears from my frantic and desperate escape from the palace. There was a tear on the right side that I could mend, and there were smudges of dirt around the hem that I was sure I could get out. It was still breathtakingly beautiful—smudges and tears and all.

I stepped back from my gown and ran my fingers through my short hair, surprised that I didn't even have any tangles; it was too short. "It will grow," the prince had said about my hair. Why had this bothered me so much? I couldn't even remember now.

I looked out the east window and saw that there was no smoke coming from Will's chimney. He must still be at the palace, caring for the guests' carriages. I hoped I would see him soon so I could thank him for all that he had done for me tonight. I hadn't even seen him or heard from him after I went to meet the prince.

It felt like a lifetime ago. It was a lifetime ago.

My eyes drooped and I swayed slightly. I shuffled over to the west window that overlooked the palace. It still blazed with light and I realized that the ball was still going on. It made me tired just thinking about it.

I yawned and walked away from the window. As I lowered my body down onto my blanket, an unexpected sob racked my body. I clutched my pillow that quickly became wet with hot tears and my breaths came in labored gasps. I wanted someone to hold me. I wanted to lay my head on someone's lap and have them caress my hair and brush the tears from my cheeks and help me make sense of everything that had happened.

I wanted my mother.

Instead, I wrapped my arms around me, trying to give myself the comfort and strength I needed. I was so exhausted. I was grieving—for more things than I even knew or understood. I felt myself drifting out of consciousness as my tears slowed and my pillow became cold and damp. I reached for my other blanket and covered me, tucking it under my feet, one of them sheathed in glass.

Refining Fire

Chapter 26

THE BRIGHT SUNLIGHT STREAMING IN MY WINDOW AND onto my face alerted me to the fact that I had slept in. I sat up with a gasp and ran to the window. The sun was high above my head. I had never slept so late in my life! Lucy must be miserable! Victoria would be irate! Why hadn't she come to punish me for my slothfulness?

Without bothering to dress, I raced down the long staircase, down the long main hall, and stopped dead in front of Victoria's door. I grasped the doorframe as I gawked at the bedroom. The bed was empty and the sheets had been removed and folded at the foot of the bed.

I had never been so disoriented in my life. Every morning I knew exactly where I was. I did my chores without complaining or wondering why. I was always acutely aware of my situation in life and had come to accept it like breathing.

My world had changed so much in one week—in one evening. I clutched onto the doorframe as I tried to comprehend it all. I reached up to touch my chopped off hair and it helped to bring me back to reality. Victoria was dead. Mabel and Cecelia were gone. Will could still be at the palace. The prince had passionately and unequivocally professed his love for me last night.

And I was alone.

Lucy! She needed to be milked. I ran down the stairs, through the kitchen, and out the back door. I threw open the barn door and was already trying to soothe the poor cow. I hoped my voice would help to calm her down before I actually tried touching her. But she wasn't there.

I ran to the barn doors, made sure no one was around, and dashed out to the pasture. There she was, innocently munching on the grass; the gate was closed behind her.

Had I milked her and taken her out and closed the gate in my sleep? I wouldn't be surprised. I ran to the chicken coop. Mary was sleeping soundly in her house, no eggs to be gathered. I ran back to the house and into the kitchen. In my haste to take care of Lucy, I hadn't seen that there were two jugs of milk on the floor and one egg sitting in a bowl on the table.

Tears filled my eyes when I realized who would have done this. Will. He had sacrificed everything for me. He had made sure I went to the ball. He had kept me safe from Victoria. He had danced with me. He had come here this morning and had taken care of my chores for me and then left quietly.

My thoughts unexpectedly turned to the prince. He had held my hand and looked passionately into my eyes. He had kissed me. I had kissed him. He knew everything about me, but hadn't pushed me away. In fact, it was only after I had told him everything that he had declared his love for me. He had offered me a life of luxury: a carefree life of ease and tranquility. He had offered me gold and jewels.

So why did a milked cow and a single egg touch my heart and bring tears to my eyes?

Because they had required sacrifice. They had required thoughtfulness. They had required love.

Will loved me.

My breath caught in my throat and my hand covered my mouth, as if keeping me from saying the words out loud. I instantly felt vain for entertaining such a notion, but immediately that feeling fled and the truth of it flowed from the top of my head to the tips of my bare toes. Will loved me.

I couldn't believe I hadn't seen it before. I thought of everything he had done for me, everything he had sacrificed and given. Every time he had made me laugh or comforted me when I wanted to crawl into a pit and never come out. His love had strengthened me, but I hadn't recognized it for what it was.

I laughed to myself, standing all alone in my kitchen, bewildered by my blindness. I wanted to run to him, to tell him . . . what? That he loved me? Would I tell him I loved him too? Did I know how to love? Did I know how to *be* loved?

I had known once.

With a small smile on my lips and a skip in my step, I stored the milk and cooked and ate my little egg. I tried in vain to control my unruly thoughts as I ate. What would it be like when I saw Will again? Would it be awkward? I didn't know what to do about this new knowledge of Will's feelings; I just knew I wanted to see him. He had never actually told me he loved me, but he had shown me, I was sure of it. The prince had told me he loved me. Had he shown me he loved me?

I thought for a moment about the time I had shared with the prince. It had been a lovely evening, for a little while, one that I would remember for the rest of my life. The prince had been witty and charming and romantic. I wondered how long he had looked for me after I so rudely ran away before he went to spend the rest of the evening with some other girl. I shook my head at this thought. He may have seemed reckless and impulsive, but he was not insincere. I had believed every word he said. I just didn't know how I felt about them.

It didn't matter now. He didn't know who I was or where to find me. It was futile even thinking about it. It had been a lovely evening, but now it was over.

I examined my immaculate kitchen. It was a very large kitchen, once used to prepare fine banquets for dozens of people. Now, there was just me, and I suddenly felt very small.

I left the kitchen, not bothering to do any of the work that needed to be done in it, and walked to the formal dining room. I remembered the huge mahogany table that used to stretch from end to end and how I used to play underneath it as a child. We would have large dinner parties and every seat would be filled with kind, laughing people. Father would be the life of the party—making jokes, telling stories, playing the violin, and making everyone feel at home.

I left the dining room and climbed up the wide staircase. I felt along the banister and the fading paint flaked off under my touch. At the top of the stairs, I stood again in the doorway of Victoria's dim room. Suddenly, I was overcome with the desire to throw open the curtains. I ran to the window and opened them wide and turned around to see if it had made a dent in the gloom. It was as if it had been set free and the charm and pleasantness of the room had returned. I would no longer dread entering this room. I picked up the neatly folded sheets on my way out so I could wash them.

I reached the end of the hall and opened the door and climbed the stairs to my tower. I noticed the squeaky fifth step and was careful not to slide my hand along the splintery wood of the banister. I opened the door at the top and walked into my tidy little bedroom. I looked out the window that faced east, where the sun would rise. It had always so kindly awoken me on those extra sleepy mornings when I had failed to wake before dawn, so that I could get my chores done and prepare breakfast before Victoria awoke. Today, it had been kind to me again and had let me get some desperately needed rest. Ever since I was young, I had always felt like the sun was watching out for me.

I looked at the tops of the huge trees that had been there for hundreds of years. They had always been comforting to me. They were the same trees that had surrounded Ashfield since it had been called Rosewood, and I felt that they knew me and my history. One of the most comforting things in those woods was the smoke that rose from Will's chimney, reminding me that I had a friend in this world.

I turned back to my little room that had been a safe haven for me. A place where no one could tell me what to do or punish me for things I had done or hadn't done. It had been my own private corner of the house where I had felt at home. Now that feeling radiated out of the room to fill every other corner of Ashfield.

It was time to live my own life now.

Chapter 27

I GOT TO WORK MOVING MY FEW BELONGINGS DOWN TO MY old bedroom—my hairbrush, some underclothing, a chipped water basin, a few blankets. My glass slipper had fallen off my foot in my sleep and I placed it back into its little blue box. I took the box and my gown and placed them in my own room—not in a crate, not under the floor.

I washed the clothes my stepsisters had left behind, grateful for the new additions to my own wardrobe. My poor gray dress was ready to retire. But my "new" clothes still had to dry and then be taken in, so it would have to last one more day.

I was upstairs, scrubbing Victoria's bedroom floor when the front door opened with a deafening crash.

"Ella!" Will cried.

I stared in the direction of the door, too stunned to move, my hands gripping the scrub brush. My heart started racing in my chest, but I didn't know if it was because I was suddenly nervous to see him or because he sounded like he was in pain.

I heard muffled footsteps and then my name being called again, this time desperation tinted his tone. I jumped up and wiped my hands on my dress and ran out of the room. He had left the foyer and I could hear him coming back into the house from the back door.

"Ella," he said again. This time he didn't call for me. He simply stated it in what sounded like despair.

I stood at the top of the stairs and watched him emerge from the doorway of the dining room. It was the first time I'd seen him since my revelation that he loved me. What if I had been wrong? I felt flustered and shy all of a sudden, not being able to find my voice. I wanted to thank him for all of his help, but somehow couldn't find the words. But the desperation in his voice erased my self-consciousness and replaced it with concern.

"Will?"

His head shot up and he gazed at me in disbelief.

"What's wrong?" I asked. I ran down the steps and stopped a few feet away from him.

"You're here?" he whispered.

"Of course I'm here. Where else would I be?" I laughed lightly. He must be exhausted. "You need to go home and rest. First, let me get you something to eat. I need to thank you for helping me this . . ." I started to walk toward the kitchen, but his hand grabbed mine. Without a word, he sat down on the bottom step, and pulled me to sit down next to him.

He looked at me for a moment, his lips pursed in thought. "Ella, I assume you've been home all day?" He sounded more than merely curious.

I nodded. "Yes. I have had so much to get done here." I paused, not sure how he'd take the next thing I had to say. "Victoria died last night," I muttered.

"Pity," he said with a smile.

I understood his reaction—he had seen me hurt at her hand countless times and had felt helpless against it for years. He had seen my whip marks, my cheeks stained from tears, and even the way I hung my head after being in her presence.

"Will, something happened to me last night," I began. I didn't quite know how to say it.

He nodded solemnly. "At the ball?" he guessed. I shook my head. I didn't want to talk about the ball. There were too many dreams and nightmares mingled in one memory.

"No, I mean with Victoria. Will, as she lay dying, I saw her for the first time. Really saw her. All her walls were down, whether she wanted them to be or not. She simply didn't have the strength to keep them up anymore. She was frail and weak and vulnerable, like she finally needed someone to care for her and could admit it. Her daughters had said good-bye and didn't shed a tear for her. It . . . it broke my heart. Truly broke it. I forgave her. She squeezed my hand." My voice trembled.

Will's familiar look of wonder returned again as he listened to me. "The prince doesn't deserve you. No one deserves you."

"The prince? What are you talking about? I was just telling you about something that happened to me, that's all." I tried to sound casual, but there was a note of defensiveness in my voice.

"That's my point. You *allowed* it to happen to you. You let yourself forgive. That doesn't just happen."

There was something else bothering him; I could see it. He must have seen the questions in my eyes because he pursed his lips again and thought for a moment. "Well, Ella. It seems that you made quite an impression on the prince last night."

I wanted to look away to hide the blush that crept onto my cheeks, but I didn't want to look guilty. "Oh? How do you know that?" My voice was an octave too high to sound nonchalant.

"Well, it's all over the kingdom that the prince fell in love last night." Will was looking more penetratingly at me than he ever had. I dropped my eyes and looked at the stones beneath my feet.

"Oh?" I said again. I wasn't even fooling myself. I sounded utterly guilty. "He fell in love?"

"Love," Will repeated the word as if it were repulsive to him.

I was desperate to change the topic of conversation. "Why were you looking for me?"

He searched my eyes for a moment in somber silence. "Ella," he said softly. "Did you lose a slipper last night?"

"Yes!" I exclaimed. "Did someone find it? I thought I'd never see . . ." My voice trailed off at the expression on his face.

"Yes, someone found it. The prince," Will said. I knew there was more to it than that, but he seemed to want an explanation of why and how my shoe had come off my foot—my mother's shoe that Will knew I loved.

"Yes, I lost my shoe." I sighed, knowing he deserved the truth, but it didn't make it any easier to say. "The prince told me he loved me last night. He proposed. He . . . he kissed me." I paused, my face burning so hot I thought I would burst into flames. *Why* did it have to be Will I told all of this to?

"Hmm. So he proposed and your shoe fell off?" I could hear a smile in his voice, though I couldn't meet his eyes to see if I was right.

I laughed. "No. I . . . I ran away and his guards chased me and I lost my shoe. I didn't even stop to pick it up," I ended with sadness.

Will deliberated again and grimaced. "Ella, about your shoe . . . The prince went looking to find the owner of that glass slipper and when he does . . . he's going to marry her."

"What! How is he going to do that?" I cried.

"He is already doing it. He started early this morning, going from house to house, trying the glass slipper on each and every maiden in the kingdom."

"But . . . but what if it fits more than one person?" I asked.

"That's a very good question," Will answered.

I was trying desperately to grasp the enormity of what Will had said. "Will, is that why you were looking for me? To see if the slipper fit me?"

He nodded slowly. I could tell there was something else he wasn't saying. He stood slowly off the step and reached out his hand and I put mine in his. He gently pulled me up to face him and wrapped his arm around me, more to steady me than to embrace me. "Word is out all over the kingdom," he whispered. "The slipper fit someone and the prince is taking her to the palace as we speak. I thought you were gone."

Chapter 28

I WAITED FOR THE GRIEF AND INJUSTICE TO CRUSH ME. I waited for tears and the anger and the sadness. But nothing came. I didn't feel numb; I didn't feel the pain that would make me want to feel numb.

I wondered if my lack of distress was because I had already figured I had lost the prince the night before. I had fled from him—impolitely and improperly, yet willingly—without really knowing the reason why. Or perhaps it was because the prince had already found someone else, and that gave me the freedom to do the same.

It made sense for me to be disappointed. It made sense for me to be upset. But the only thought I could grasp at was the concern that I would never get to see my slipper again. What good was one without the other—for me or for the girl the other slipper fit? I wondered if there was something wrong with me. Why was I worried about such a seemingly trivial thing?

I looked up at Will's face and saw that he had been studying mine intently. "Ella, tell me what you're thinking. You don't seem upset. Don't act calm just because I'm here. It won't hurt my feelings if you're disappointed." He said the words sincerely, but I heard a hint of doubt in his voice. "He's the prince. I understand that. He could have given you everything."

He stopped himself. He probably thought I'd lost the ability to speak. Perhaps I had.

In reaction to whatever Will saw on my face, his own face softened. He raised his hand and touched my arm. "Ella," he whispered. I looked up into his eyes and felt every care I'd ever had drift away into nothingness. I felt the now-familiar something spark inside of me that I felt in front of the fire two nights before. He glanced down at my lips, but this time he didn't look away.

Before I could put a name to what I was feeling, there was a faint rumbling in the distance. It sounded like a carriage, no, many carriages—dozens of carriages. The house shook faintly and the chandelier danced lightly in the air above us. I looked at Will in confusion and he looked at me in unashamed anguish. He bent his head down and pressed his lips tenderly to my cheek.

"He's coming for you. It's you he wants." He dropped his hand and walked slowly away. I heard the back door close softly.

***

THE RUMBLING CAME TO A STOP AND THE OMINOUS SILENCE that followed was palpable. I hadn't moved since Will walked out the back door, except to touch my fingers to the place his lips had touched my cheek. I was trying to figure out why he had left me. Did he want me to marry the prince? Did he not love me after all?

A brisk knock at the door brought me back to my senses, and I walked forward and opened it mechanically. As soon as I opened the door, the man who had knocked took one large step backward and with a nasal voice announced,

"His Royal Highness, Prince Kenton." As soon as he spoke I recognized him as the little man who had announced the prince in town just last week. He stepped aside and directly behind him stood the prince. He had a downcast expression on his beautiful face, and I felt a wave of pity for him. I also felt confused. Will had said the slipper fit someone else. Why had the prince come here?

I curtsied as low as I could and then opened the door wider. The prince removed his feathered hat and stepped forward into the house. I recognized Sir Thomas close behind him. I smiled at him and he nodded his acknowledgement. I assumed he would follow the prince into the house, but I was surprised to see him close the door once the prince was inside, leaving us alone in the foyer. The prince stood motionless and silent.

"Your Highness," I said, curtsying again. I stood up straight and looked into his face. I could see him trying to reconcile the elegantly dressed lady he had talked to last night with the girl dressed in rags smelling of hay who stood before him now.

"Is it you?" he asked. "It's really true, then? You are a servant here—in your own home?"

"Yes, Your Highness," I answered simply. I wondered if he really hadn't believed me last night, or if seeing it in real life was as difficult to grasp as it seemed.

"And where is your stepmother?" he asked, taking a step closer to me.

"She died last night, Your Highness," I answered.

"Oh. I'm sorry. Are you sad?" he asked kindly. He must have remembered how I described her last night.

"I am sad that we did not get along better while she was alive. I wish we had had more time to understand each other." I was being as plain and honest as I possibly could. He didn't need to know every detail.

He nodded in understanding. "Ella Blakeley. Is that your name?"

"Yes, Your Highness." I wondered who had told him, but I didn't feel at liberty to ask.

"Ella," he whispered to himself as he closed his eyes. He smiled and slowly opened his eyes and took a step closer, his demeanor becoming less formal. "Why did you leave me last night? I have been tormented."

The horror I felt at the memory of how I had abandoned him returned and I ducked my head in shame. He deserved an explanation.

"I don't know if I can explain it. It doesn't make sense even to me."

"Please try," he whispered.

I sighed. "I was confused." I took a step back and turned away from him. "Everything happened so fast. You . . . you told me you loved me. How is that possible? How can you want to marry me? You don't know me."

I heard him take a step forward. He placed his hands on my shoulders and turned me to face him. "Ella. You told me all about yourself last night. I do know you and I love everything about you. I want to take care of you. I want to give you everything—a beautiful life surrounded by the most charming things life could offer. You'll never have to serve another person for as long as you live. It sounds like you have earned that right. You've suffered for so long. Forget all of that sadness and heartache. Leave all that behind and come with me." He tenderly stroked my cheek with the back of his fingers. "I love you. Truly. From the first moment I saw you in the palace courtyard, I knew that your place was next to me on the throne."

For a moment, I could see it. I could see myself in my beautiful gown; my glass slippers peeking out from under my hem; my hair grown out and piled high on my head;

my hands soft and clean with no dirt under my fingernails or calluses on my palms. I could almost smell the perfume and taste the delectable food. I sat next to my handsome prince and he held my hand and looked at me adoringly. It was everything any girl would want . . . and should want, I told myself.

"Your stepmother is dead. Where are your stepsisters?"

"They left after she died," I answered.

He nodded, a look of triumph in his face. "You don't have to take care of them anymore. There's nothing here for you," he said.

He was right. My parents were gone. Victoria was gone. Cecelia and Mabel were gone. Will's face flashed through my mind. If I was being honest, Will was one of the main reasons I was not riding away with the prince that very moment.

The prince must have seen something in my expression. "There is someone else, isn't there?"

I looked away. "Nothing's ever happened between us. He's a friend. A very good friend." My voice trembled and tears threatened. "We're the same. We help each other. We support each other . . ."

"You love each other?"

The thought had entered my mind, but I had never allowed myself to think about it long enough to believe if it was true or not. All my life I had thought that Will was kind and charitable and helpful, and that he even felt sorry for me—that those were the reasons he was always helping me. But the changes that had occurred during the past week between us had begun to open my eyes to the possibility that perhaps there could be something more between us. And just this morning, I had come to the conclusion that he truly did love me. I had been too afraid to admit that I might love him too. But hearing the words out loud made it impossible to deny.

I nodded slowly. "Yes, Your Highness. I love him." The truth of my words overwhelmed me.

He took another step closer and I had to tip my head up to see his eyes. He reached out his hand and took mine and looked intensely into my eyes. "Could you love me too?"

I smiled up at him and the sincerity on his face. How could I not love someone who loved me in spite of my dirty face, roughened hands, and short hair? He had kissed me. He was handsome and wealthy. He would take care of me. But there were two things that were bothering me. I decided to ask him about the most urgent one.

"Your Highness, didn't my glass slipper fit someone else?" I asked the question as gently as I could so it didn't sound like I was scolding him. Somewhere out there was a girl whose foot had fit the slipper and the prince had said that he would marry that girl. I wondered how she felt now, knowing that it was not her he had been searching for.

He looked chagrined. "Yes." He shook his head. "I didn't know your name or where you lived. Your slipper was the one thing I was sure would lead me to you. It was the tiniest, daintiest thing I had ever seen. I couldn't imagine it fitting anyone else!" He sighed and hung his head miserably. "I've created quite a mess."

"May I ask where the girl is?" I asked.

He pursed his lips and kept his eyes on the floor, deliberating. He slowly lifted his eyes. "She's outside in the carriage."

I tried to hide my astonishment. I felt terrible for the poor girl sitting out there. She must know that the prince was trying to figure out a way out of his predicament, out of having to marry her. "Does she know who I am?" I asked, trying to keep my voice under control.

He nodded slowly. "She's your best friend. Jane Emerson."

I swallowed hard and tried to keep my face calm, but I knew the countless conflicting emotions I felt played like an open book on my face. My first feeling of shock was quickly replaced by clarity. Jane and I had always joked about our tiny feet. Of course she would be the only other woman the slipper would fit. Next was anger. She had been the one who had told Victoria I was at the ball, and it was written plainly on her face as we passed in the courtyard that she had meant it to be vindictive, though she might not have fully grasped the possible repercussions. From what Jane was told, I was supposed to be sick at home, not next in line after her to meet the prince, and she must have resented me for that.

I fought against my next emotion but knew it would come anyway. Compassion filled my heart and crowded out all the anger, as it always does. Jane had loved the prince from that first day in town. She was lovely and regal and just as deserving as anyone. She had made a mistake, but it didn't define who she was. She got caught up in the excitement, and even intrigue, of the ball just like everyone else. I knew her heart and I knew she was hurting out there.

Suddenly I knew it was she who had told the prince my name, where I lived, and that the slipper belonged to me. The moment I realized this, I knew that she truly was still my friend, and now that she was out of the clutches of my stepsisters, she could see clearly. She was desperately trying to make amends. She had seen the error of her ways and would perhaps be all the wiser for it. She had been used by the same people who had hurt me and I knew her well enough to know that she would not allow something like that to happen again. I wanted so badly to run out to her and embrace her and tell her that everything was going to be fine.

The prince watched me as I took the time to figure all this out. He observed me closely as my face finally relaxed and smoothed, yet he appeared to be dissatisfied with the understanding that must be on my face. I think he would have preferred I stopped at anger.

He reached up and grasped my arms. "Ella, I love *you*." He paused to search for the right words. "I came searching for you. I know my plan to find you wasn't exactly well thought out. I know I'm impulsive. It's my worst fault. But it's you I want."

The prince reached into his pocket and retrieved my glass slipper. He knelt down chivalrously and slipped it onto my bare foot. He looked up at me and smiled tenderly. He stood slowly and gazed deeply into my eyes, a pleading expression on his attractive face. He reached a hand up to stroke my short hair that I had left undone, and then he encircled me in his arms and kissed me.

Chapter 29

The palace looked so majestic from my view out the carriage window. The sun was beginning its descent behind the hills, casting a warm, pink glow on the ancient edifice. I admired its grandeur against the picturesque scenery of the green hills behind it.

I had taken a step into the darkness and had made my choice and was now enveloped in light and joy and tranquility. I knew it didn't mean that every problem I ever had, or would have, would miraculously vanish, but I felt peace, knowing that I had chosen the life I wanted to live, the life that would make me happy—indescribably happy. I had found the man I loved and I was going to be with him forever.

I admired the luxurious fabric that lined the seats and the walls of the royal carriage with my free hand. I smiled at the prince and he smiled back, a look of contentment on his face. I felt overwhelming peace as I glanced down at the fingers entwined with mine and gave them an affectionate squeeze. Everything was finally right.

Jane also looked down at our hands clasped in undying friendship, her eyes still wet from her tearful, heartfelt apology. I laid my head on her shoulder and she rested her head on mine. I peeked over at her other hand, gripped tightly in the prince's and I saw that he was looking at their hands too, the same look of contentment from before.

Once the prince kissed me, everything became clear. I was not his, and never had been. My heart belonged to someone else and I could never deny that. It was not a coincidence in my mind that the slipper had fit Jane. It fit her in every way and she would be completely at ease in her new life in the palace.

My home would always be Ashfield. It was where I had worked and sacrificed, where I had come to realize what my true beauty was and that I didn't need extravagant clothes or shoes to make me see it. I could see it in the calluses on my hands from churning butter, in the dirt under my fingernails from digging up food I had grown in my garden. Ashfield was also where I had found someone who could see my true beauty and loved me for who I was.

I could finally put words to the second thing that was bothering me. The prince loved me in spite of the calluses and dirt. Will loved me because of them.

I had explained to the prince what a beautiful person Jane truly was and that she would make the perfect princess. She was graceful and elegant and longed for that life and it suited her. I told him that I would never be happy living in a palace. He understood that part completely.

He had graciously accepted my decision, kissed my hand, and said, "Even though it was only for one night, I'm a better man for having known you."

Then he had taken me out to see Jane and we renewed our friendship with tears and then laughter. The prince laughed with us and I saw his eyes turn from me to Jane. He saw her lovely face and saw who she really was and that she already was a princess. He asked me if there was anything he could do for me and I had only one request.

The carriage came to a stop near the pond, where I had asked to be dropped off. I embraced Jane and kissed her cheek. She made me promise again to visit her at the palace. The prince took my hand and kissed it and then clasped Jane's again. He smiled at me to let me know he was content.

I slipped my glass slipper off my foot and placed it in my apron pocket. I poked my head out the open door of the carriage and saw the footman there to help me down. I ignored him and impulsively hopped out of the carriage. I raced as fast as my feet would carry me. I could hear the quiet laughter of Jane and Prince Kenton fading behind me.

***

I RELISHED IN THE DELICIOUS CRUNCH OF THE NEWLY FALLEN leaves beneath my feet as they swirled behind me as I raced through the trees. I didn't have far to run, but it was still too far. I hoped and prayed Will would be at the pond. It had always been the place where we could find each other. I laughed as I realized that I had loved him for so long. I couldn't even remember not loving him. I had always sought his comfort and strength, always knew he'd be there to lift me when I was falling, to make me laugh when I wanted to cry.

I heard the gently swaying cattails over my wildly beating heart and I slowed to a walk. I came to the clearing in the trees where we usually met in the mornings. Sometimes he would bring me firewood; sometimes I would bring him bread. I sighed and smiled at my blindness.

I cast my eyes across the glassy water and saw him. He was sitting on the ground, leaning against his favorite tree. His eyes were fastened on me. He must have heard my chaotic dash through the forest. I glanced over at my usual spot on the moist banks and kept walking. And for the first time, I began to cross the bridge over to his side, not waiting for him to come to me as I always had.

He saw me crossing the bridge and surprise lit his face. He stood and walked onto the bridge to meet me in the middle. We stopped a few feet from each other. His face was a carefully guarded mask, and I realized he might be wondering what I was doing there. It seemed preposterous to me that he didn't know I loved him, but I realized I hadn't been clear on that point until recently.

"Have you come to say good-bye?" he asked. The mask fell away, and I saw the pain he wasn't able to conceal anymore.

His eyes widened in wonder as I raised my arms and placed both my hands on the sides of his strong face. "Never," I whispered passionately.

He stood completely motionless for a moment. Then he closed his eyes and raised his hands to place them over mine. When he opened his eyes, the fire had returned. The tenderness in his eyes was mingled with an intensity that made me tremble. His hands traced down my arms to my shoulders, along my back and then wrapped tightly around my waist and held me close to him. I smiled at him and nodded slightly.

"I'm yours," I said.

He beamed back at me, leaned down, and pressed his lips to mine. My heart pounded in my chest and I truly began to let myself feel . . . to live, to love, and to be loved. What I hadn't known as I had protected myself for all those years against feeling real pain was that I had also been denying myself the opportunity to feel real happiness. I finally knew that by allowing myself to feel completely, that I would also be allowing myself to love completely, and I was ready.

When the prince had kissed me at the ball, I couldn't even remember my own name. When Will kissed me, it was as if I finally knew who I was.

Slowly, Will released me and buried his face in my hair. "Ella, I thought I lost you! The prince came to marry you and take you away from me. He has everything to offer you and I have nothing. I can't believe you're standing here. Do you realize that you just said no to a prince?" he asked, slowly shaking his head back and forth, his lips brushing against my cheek.

"No, I didn't," I said and held him tighter.

He chuckled. "Ella, I realize you know this and it's not that I want you to change your mind, but you could have been a princess—a queen—in a palace! The prince obviously loves you and wanted you, yet here you are. Please explain this to me."

I pulled back so I could see every fleck of gold in his green eyes. "This wasn't just a choice between two lives. This was a choice between two loves."

"Love?" The repulsion from earlier when Will said that word was replaced by warmth.

I nodded. "The prince told me he loved me last night. He promised me a life of ease and comfort and luxury. He stayed awake all night and searched for me all day. And I will admit, I was flattered." I paused, overwhelmed by the clarity I felt. "The prince swept me off my feet, but you planted my feet firmly on the ground."

Will smiled and touched his forehead to mine.

I smiled back at him and continued. "You have sacrificed for me. You have given so much. You have suffered when I've suffered. I saw pain in your eyes for my pain. You have shared my joys and have always been there to give me comfort and friendship. This is the kind of love I need. I don't need someone to take me out of the fire so I don't get burned; I need someone to walk through the flames with me. And I will do the same for you."

My voice caught and I couldn't say any more. I was in absolute awe of him. He had respected me enough to wait for me to come back to life so that I could feel again and let myself love again. He had even unselfishly stepped aside and given me the opportunity to fall in love with a prince, knowing that I could have been taken away, but wanting me to be happy.

I laughed softly. "How could I have been so blind?"

He laughed gently and held me close as he whispered in my ear, "I would have waited forever."

All I could do was nod and try to blink back the tears. I knew he would have.

"Ella," he murmured. My name sounded so beautiful on his lips, his voice low and soft.

"Yes?" I smiled.

He pulled back so he could look at me. "I want to offer you everything I have. I will do all I can to make you safe and comfortable and happy. It won't happen all at once, but we're going to make it. I know it can never compete with a palace and jewels and gold, but . . ."

I stopped him with a kiss. "There's no competition."

He grinned back at me, though I could still see a bit of uncertainty in his eyes.

"Will, all I need is you. When you told me that night by the fire that you had nothing to offer me, you were wrong. You are everything to me."

He gently lifted both my hands, kissed my palms, closed his eyes, and whispered my name. I felt my tears roll down my cheeks and he kissed them.

"Will," I whispered.

He looked at my face, which he cradled tenderly in his hands. He smiled at me, knowing what I was going to say and I knew he felt the same way.

"I love you," we finally declared after years of waiting. We laughed softly together.

"Then it must be true," I said.

Will kissed me again and then reached for my hand,

which I placed eagerly in his. With my other hand, I reached into my apron pocket and felt my glass slipper. As we stood together on our rickety little bridge overlooking the pond, I reflected on the breathtaking view I had of the entire kingdom from the grand palace balcony where I had stood with the prince. From that magnificent vantage point, I could see my past and present, and I had wondered if I could see my future. I hadn't realized it then, but my past, present, and future were all within my grasp, in the hand I now held in mine.

Epilogue

Ella dug her hands in the soft soil, reveling in its richness. She pulled out a perfectly formed potato and placed it in her basket with a satisfied smile. She stood and pushed her long braid behind her shoulders so that it fell down her back and then she brushed the dirt off her long, dark blue dress.

"I'll take that, ma'am." Maude reached out for Ella's basket of potatoes. "You know I can do this, ma'am." Maude smiled and gestured to the garden and all the work they had just done.

"Thank you, Maude." Ella smiled in return as she handed Maude her basket. "But you know I love to do it." Maude nodded and carried both hers and Ella's baskets into the kitchen. Ella looked out over the distant hills. Will and Peter should be back soon from their ride. She held up her skirts as she carefully stepped around the tender plants and paused at the very edge of the garden. She knelt down in front of the four headstones there, kissed her fingers, and touched them to each stone. The tender blades of grass hadn't completely grown over the freshest grave and she lovingly stroked the soil, and let a few tears soak into it.

She let out a quiet sob, dried her cheeks with her clean corner of her apron, and sighed. She stood and walked over to the stable where the loud neighing of the horses frightened the birds off the roof. Patrick had just brought them in from their peaceful afternoon of grazing lazily in the sun.

"Good evening, Patrick," Ella said as their head stableman walked around the corner with a bucket of oats.

Patrick's wrinkled face lit up as he waved enthusiastically. "Good evening to you, ma'am!" He strode over to one of the stalls. "Peaches' foot is healing up nicely. She should be good as new next month."

"That's wonderful news, Patrick. You and Will are miracle workers!" Ella cried.

Patrick's tan skin glowed and he ducked his head. Ella laughed and stepped closer to the stall nearest to her. She affectionately stroked Old Charlie Horse's soft nose and patted the subtly sagging skin under his chin. She gave him a handful of oats from the bucket and stepped out of the stable and to the barn. The cows were getting their evening milking as they chomped lazily on their hay. Ella's eyes fell on the stall that had once been Lucy's. Ella would never forget how that sweet cow had kept her and her family alive for so many years, especially during that first winter after she and Will were married. Ella absently rubbed her stomach, remembering the piercing hunger. Then she smiled at the memory of how blissfully happy they were even in the midst of their poverty.

Ella left the barn and made her way to the front yard. She passed the chicken coop, smiled at the clucking of the happily gossiping chickens, and tossed them a handful of corn. When she reached the front yard, she stood and admired the glorious roses that framed Ashfield. They were more beautiful than they had ever been. She cut various colored blooms and brought them inside. As she opened the heavy oak doors, the screeching sounds of a young girl learning to play the violin filled the air.

Ella entered the drawing room. Tears filled her eyes as she looked at her daughter standing in the rosy glow of the sunset, her violin on her shoulder, her bow jerkily moving back and forth across the strings. Ella slowly walked past the settee and stepped gingerly onto the rug that Elizabeth stood on.

"It sounds beautiful, sweetheart," Ella whispered as she kissed the top of her daughter's head. She smelled like sunshine.

Elizabeth dropped her bow and beamed up at her mother. "Thank you, Mama! It's Grandfather's favorite!"

"And you played it beautifully, darling. I'm sure he could hear it from heaven." Ella kissed her one more time, and Elizabeth went back to her practicing, focusing on playing the music now and not just the notes.

On her way out of the room, Ella glanced down at Ruth Haywood's most recent letter sitting on the drawing room table and smiled. Ever since the night of the ball, Ella had come to love and know Ruth as Ella had always longed to love and know her own mother. Aunt Ruth, as the children called her, would be coming to visit next month and everyone was delighted, especially Ella. She walked from the drawing room, through the formal living room, the foyer, the dining room with its white wallpaper with tiny forget-me-nots painted into the pattern, and into the kitchen. It was bustling with energy as the cooks prepared the evening meal. They smiled up at their mistress, and Ella smiled back.

"They should be home shortly. Thank you for keeping everything warm a little longer." Ella breathed deeply. "It smells absolutely delicious in here," she complimented.

"Of course it does," said Maude with a broad smile. "It's your recipe!"

Ella grinned back as she made her way to the cupboard that held the vases, careful to stay out of the way of the bustling cooks, and lifted out her favorite one. It wasn't extravagant, but it was precious to her. Will had brought Ella her first bouquet of flowers in it soon after she told him she was going to have their first baby. She smiled tenderly as she placed the flowers in the vase and filled it with water from the well.

As she carried the flowers upstairs, Ella ran her free hand along the glassy smooth whiteness of the banister. She stopped when she reached the first door at the top of the stairs and walked inside. Elizabeth's room was one of the cheeriest rooms in the house. Ella placed the flowers on the table next to Elizabeth's bed. She heard a soft wailing from the nursery down the hall.

Ella quickly left the room, walked to the nursery door, and quietly pushed it open. Little Henry had wiggled out of his blankets and was flinging his clenched fists in the air. Ella gently scooped him up and held him lovingly against her shoulder. Henry immediately calmed down and turned his head to her cheek.

"Are you hungry, little baby?" Ella crooned. She carried him to the wooden rocking chair in the corner by the window and fed him while he wrapped his dimpled hand around her finger. She smiled down at him and stroked his chubby legs and arms that were finally filling out. He had been such a tiny little thing when he was born. His twin brother had been even smaller and tragically had not survived delivery. It had broken Ella and Will's hearts in two, mourning the death of one little one while rejoicing in the survival of the other. They had held each other on the bed and wept together in agony and in joy.

Little Henry dozed as he nursed, but his tiny fingers still held Ella's tightly. After rocking him and patting his back for a moment, she carried him down the stairs and stood to look out the tall window that overlooked the stables. Ella heard the sound of hooves before she could actually see the horses and their riders. But when they emerged from behind the hill, a brilliant smile lit Ella's face. She turned and the governess was standing behind her with a knowing smile.

"I'll take him, ma'am," she said as she held out her arms. Ella tenderly kissed Henry's fuzzy head, gingerly transferred him to Molly's arms, and then dashed to the kitchen and out the back door.

Will pulled his horse to a stop and was followed closely by Peter on his smaller horse. Before Will's horse had completely stopped, Will jumped off and ran to Ella, picking her up in his arms and twirling her around.

"Oh, I missed you, my darling!" Will exclaimed.

Ella laughed breathlessly. "You've only been gone for a few hours." She kissed him. "But I know exactly how you feel."

Will placed Ella back on the ground and kissed her hand. "We saw Jane and Kenton while we were riding. They invited us over for supper tomorrow."

"Wonderful!" Ella exclaimed. It had been three months since she had seen her friend. Jane had come to comfort Ella when her baby had died and to meet Little Henry.

Jane and the Prince were a beautiful couple with two adorable children. It had been delightful and satisfying to watch their love grow over the years and see how perfect they were together.

Peter overheard the conversation between his parents. "We're going to Anne's tomorrow?" he asked with a scowl. "She always pulls my hair," he said as he absently rubbed his head. Princess Anne was a year younger than Peter and was a bit of a tease.

Ella laughed and reached over to tousle his brown curls

and Peter's face reddened. "Aw, Mama!" he said as he playfully pushed her hand away.

"You're just too handsome for your own good, Pete," she said, laughing. He blushed more deeply. "Where's my hug, young man? I've barely seen you all day!" He laughed and threw his arms around his mother and she kissed the top of his head. "Go wash up for dinner."

Peter ran to the well, and Will came to stand by Ella's side. He took her hand. "We didn't miss dinner?" he said with relief. He kissed her cheek. "Thank you for waiting for us."

Ella gazed up at the man who had brought her back to life; who had starved with her in the early days of their marriage; who had laughed with her and cried with her and worked alongside her; who dreamed with her and strived to realize those dreams.

For a moment, she pictured her wedding gown that hung safely in her wardrobe, and the glass slippers that sat protected in their box beneath her gown. The first time she wore them, she was just beginning to see who she really was. The next time she wore them, she was a bride, marrying the man who had seen her for who she was all along. He made her feel like a princess and he would always be her prince.

She reached up her hand to touch Will's face. "I would have waited forever," she whispered.

Acknowledgments

First, I want to thank my Heavenly Father for blessing me with a love of words. I hope I have used them well. Also, for blessing me with people and experiences in my life that have taught me so much.

Thank you to my sweet Gary who has been unfailingly supportive and encouraging, for believing in me when I decided to do this crazy thing, and for showing me what true love looks like—always in all ways.

Thank you to my five adorable, sweet, hilarious, boys: Andrew, Ryan, Benjamin, Spencer, and Joseph. Thank you for supporting me and cheering me on. Someday I'll write a "boy book" just for you. I love you so much it feels like my heart is going to explode.

Thank you to my amazing parents. Thank you Mom for listening to me for hours as I tried to figure out what in the world I was doing and why, and for being my number one cheerleader. Thank you Dad for your encouragement and for your photography, videography, editing, and audio expertise and your tireless (or very tired) hours helping me. I totally lucked out in the parent department. I love you!

Thank you to my amazing siblings: Robert, Jennifer, Angelyn, Kristine, Edward, and Carolyn. I love you more than I can say. To celebrate, let's have popcorn and Orange Julius and watch home movies, or we can have Dad's pancakes, bacon, and eggs. I'll bring the shower caps! Thank you also to my siblings-in-law: Kristina, Josh, Shawn, Spencer, Lindsey, and Doug for your help and support. I owe you all cinnamon rolls and Danishes for years.

Thank you to my wonderful in-laws: George, Jean, Ann, Kelley, Tina, Lynn, Stephanie, Mark, Miranda, and Heidi for your love and support. I love you!

Thank you Natalie for being my beta reader before I knew there was such a thing, and for helping me keep writing even when it was plain old hard. I love you, Buddy!

Thank you my sweet Marilee for reading *Ella* and loving and understanding her from the very first horrendous draft. I love you, friend. I'll meet you at the fence!

Thank you to Hannah Ballard for loving *Ella* from the very beginning and sending me beautiful emails that made me (and my husband and my mom and neighbor) cry for joy.

Thank you my dear Emma Parker for your incredible editing skills and for being the speediest email-sender-backer in the West! Thank you for your help and encouragement and friendship. We're totally kindred spirits.

Thank you Greg Martin and Kelly Martinez for your invaluable help with marketing.

Thank you Rebecca Greenwood, Michelle May, and the design team for the breathtakingly beautifully perfectly perfect cover. I sure hope people judge the book by it.

Thank you Melissa Caldwell and Sarah Barlow, for helping me polish *Ella* until my brain hurt . . . but it was so worth it. You are meticulously brilliant!

Thank you Anne Shirley, Jo March, Elizabeth Bennet, and Jane Eyre. You continue to inspire.